The Devil is an Irishman

The Devil is an Irishman

EDDIE LENIHAN

MERCIER PRESS

WHAT YOU NEED TO READ

MERCIER PRESS

Cork

www.mercierpress.ie

Trade enquiries to CMD Distribution
55A Spruce Avenue, Stillorgan Industrial Park,
Blackrock, County Dublin

© Eddie Lenihan 1995

ISBN: 978 1 85635 566 7

15 14 13 12 11 10 9 8 7 6 5

A CIP record for this title is available from the British Library

 Mercier Press receives financial assistance from the Arts
Council/An Chomhairle Ealaíon

Printed and bound in the EU

Contents

Introduction

If the Devil is no Irishman, he surely deserves to be, because from time immemorial he has frequented the land of Ireland, held constant and intimate commerce with the people of Ireland and shown every sign of attachment to both the country and its population. If this does not entitle him to at least honorary Irish citizenship there is little in the way of justice in this world – or the next.

The Devil stories I have collected here are a mere four out of hundreds in existence. The fact that there are so many to choose from proves beyond reasonable doubt that the Dark One has been a focus of Irish attention for centuries – he is one of our own, almost.

An odd fact, but one not entirely to be wondered at, is that Devil stories far outnumber tales about his opposite number – God – in Irish tradition. Can it be that we Irish are in some fallen way more comfortable with the infernal than with the celestial?

I think it can.

Certain it is that the Devil, as seen in Irish stories, is a familiar sort of fellow, who may give you fair play if you can display a flash of wit or a dash of courage at the appropriate time, one indeed who is susceptible to a wide range of human weaknesses such as swearing, gambling, drinking, pride particularly – but not sex! The more one considers it the more it reads like the profile of a fine specimen of Irishness!

And in this lies perhaps the most unpalatable truth of all (as well as the beginning of ultimate hope): we, each one of us, contain in ourselves the Devil, as he does his best to accommodate us. Whether the same is true of our relationship with God is perhaps harder to tell ... But that is a story for another time and place.

Suffice it to say for now that without these tales, passed down from generation to generation, our lives, our culture would be much the poorer. It is to try to convince you, the reader, that this is so that I bring this sample of stories together here for your scrutiny.

Believe them. Enjoy them. Because they are nothing if not the truth.

The Two-Rooted Briar

Not another county in Ireland has more gamblers to
the square mile than County Clare. And not everyday gamblers, either, but seasoned card-sharpers. Never has a farmer at
the mart of Ennis, Kilfenora, Kilrush or Sixmilebridge been
known to show up without a deck in his hind pocket. And in
more than one Clare parish the priest has had to stop in the
middle of Sunday Mass and step down from the altar to break
up the game at the church door when it became so noisy that
the congregation could no longer concentrate on their prayers.
And no bridal suite of any hotel worthy of the name in the
Banner County but is equipped with at least one deck, in
case the newly-weds should wish to amuse themselves. Such
is the love they have for the Devil's Prayerbook in County
Clare – at work, at play and at prayer. In few other parts of
Ireland are men and women to be found more dedicated to
their trade.

It is hardly surprising, therefore, that within the county
there should be fierce rivalries between baronies, parishes and
even townlands in the matter of card-playing. For example,
the Moyasta Maulers rarely saw eye-to-eye with the Lahinch
Losers (not a name of their own choosing, this; but therein lies
another tale entirely), nor did the Scariff Stealers ever yield,
except in extremity, to the Clarecastle Cabaires; and to think
that the Ruan Rooters would look anywhere except down on
all-comers – including the Clonderlaw Cleaners, who claimed
to represent everywhere west of Kilrush – was to invite ridi-
cule. And so it went in every part of the county, challenge and

reply, insult and counter-insult – and all in the name of good clean sport and traditional ways.

In only one place did the players feel no need of a fierce-sounding name to intimidate their foes, and that because their reputation was there already for all to reflect on. That place was Ballinruan, close by Crusheen on the Ennis–Gort highway. From this high, poor and rocky outpost the inhabitants had for generations defied the worst attempts of the lawbringers of the empire and had survived in their precarious holdings mainly on the proceeds of their sorties into the lowlands on gambling expeditions. Professional to a man, they were – and are to this day! In that place no man would be allowed to sit in to a serious game of cards – and every game to them was, by its very definition, serious – until he had served seven years at learning all the rules and subtle niceties, including the tokens in all their wondrous variety. Yes, tokens. For all the gamblers in that part of the world had their own collection of signs and signals: two winks of the left eye meant the ace of hearts. A scratch on the right side of the nose: the king of clubs. Two short slurps while drinking a pint of porter: the joker was in hand, waiting to flatten the five of trumps that was expected to clear all before it. And so on, down to the miserable Tulla Hearse, the ten of clubs.

Yet if this fact had been mentioned to any of those seasoned players, if some poor innocent had accused them of cheating, a fight would be liable to break out immediately, honour at stake.

'Cheatin'? What the hell are you talkin' about? Aren't they all doin' it? What chance has the man that don't?'

A hard question to answer, in truth.

Now, in that very parish of Ballinruan there was a man living who was known to one and all as Martin the Cards. Easy to know what his calling in life was; even his original surname had become largely forgotten because of it. Without a shadow of doubt, his like was not in the seven parishes round about when it came to making a deck whistle. No man had a stricter or a longer apprenticeship served to the same cards than he; as capable a man as ever fingered a deck – all of it learned on long winter nights in places like Barefield, Kilanena, Tubber and on out into the wilds of Kilbe-a-canty and Kinvara, where a man's life was worth only the next trick, if even that. But – and such things sometimes happen – he was an honest man, like his father and grandfather before him; no tokens for him.

'Play'em as you find'em or don't play at all,' were his father's last words to Martin on his death-bed. (No fingering rosary-beads for him; business to the very end.) And heeded he was.

But despite all his honesty a year came when things began to go against Martin at the table. And strange to say it started nowhere near the cards. First of all was the price of cattle; by the month of June they could hardly be given away as presents, and by September farmers were releasing them along the roads, hoping they might go on their rambles and not be eating the morsel of hay that people might need to feed themselves come Christmas if things continued so – if they had any hay left, that is – because the rain started to fall in July, and worse it got from then to Lá Samhna, November Eve. Lakes rose where even the oldest of the old people remembered nothing except dry ground; thatched cottages were seen floating by on the flooded rivers with people sitting on the roofs smoking their pipes as if this was an everyday occurrence and nothing to get upset about; the sun became a vague memory, to be mulled over as people sat on their kitchen tables at night watching the rising water and hoping that it might be kind and not drown them all before morning.

The only thing that continued as before, unchanged, was the nightly card-game, and if currachs and coracles made their appearance in parts of Clare where they had never previously been seen it was through sheer necessity, for if the game died all worthwhile civilisation would come to an end and the people might as well go drown themselves – which many did in any case trying to get to their old familiar places of play.

If Martin and his neighbours had done the sensible thing and stayed at home in Ballinruan and played for the moment among themselves in that hilly place until the worst of the weather had passed and Doon Lough had returned to its accustomed level who knows what might have been the final result? But sense is one thing, the traditions and habits of a lifetime another entirely. They struggled to keep to the old routine: Monday in Barefield, Tuesday in Crusheen, Wednesday in Ruan and so on. But the chore of getting to these lowlands began to take its toll. Martin's attention began to waver, then slip – a matter of little consequence in, for example, a game of poker, where no one would suffer except himself, but a serious affair where there were two partners also to be taken into account.

They noticed, naturally, and were not slow in telling him: 'Here, blast it! What d'you mean by not hittin' that tray o' clubs an' it comin' in to you? Are you blind, or what, or is it so you think you're playin' by yourself? Wake up, man.'

That kind of talk, especially some of it from players with years less experience than him, was no help to his concentration. But worse by far were the post-mortems after each round of games. Eyes began to be averted from him and whispered comments shared that he knew were aimed at him and him alone.

His errors became so bad at last that his partners abandoned him. It happened one Friday night, in Clarecastle. He was approaching the door of the pub when he heard the muttering and scuffling inside, then a door slam. When he entered no one looked in his direction as they would normally do, to greet him; instead there was an embarrassed silence, broken only by a yelp of welcome from the publican. But it was a forced jollity. Martin knew that. He was not a fool. And he knew, too, that the slamming door he had heard was his partners stampeding out to avoid him. They were probably cringeing, praying silent prayers, in the toilet now, and for an instant he was tempted to call their bluff and go visit. But no. It was hardly worth it. He was not wanted, and the part that hurt most was that he could hardly find it in himself to blame them. He would probably do the same thing himself.

He turned, without a word, and trudged home through the darkness and rain, his mood matching the weather, knowing full well that he would get the same reception tomorrow night in Ballyea and on Sunday night in Lissycasey if he had so little self-respect as to show his face. And his wife, Cáit, knew it when he booted in the door before him. They were not usually a couple who talked much about their emotions or personal woes, a normal enough state of affairs at that time in Ireland, but necessity is a surly master, and within a very few minutes a cup of tea and a kind word or two brought all of Martin's sorrows tumbling out.

She listened, not at all amazed. Such things were by no means uncommon, she knew, sensible woman that she was.

'All right,' she soothed when he had said his piece. 'If you'll be said by me, there's only one way to get over this – apart from staying at home entirely, that is.' She smiled briefly as she added this and gave him a quick glance from the corner of her eye. But he did not notice the appeal.

He snuffled, then looked up at her.

'What is it you're blabbering about, woman? How would there be a way out o' this? I'm finished – done! – an' that's all about it. I'll go to an early grave if things don't change quick, but how would they? The damage is done an' that's that.'

He was not a pretty sight just then, whining. Cáit felt like giving him a boot in a strategical place, to bring him back to something resembling a man, even if only briefly.

'Will you catch a hold o' yourself?' She snorted, goaded by his weakness. 'Are you my husband or a ciaróg?'

'I don't know any more, an' that's the truth of it,' he whimpered, a defeated specimen of humanity.

'Listen to me now,' she hissed, 'an' listen very carefully. I always heard it said by my people in west Clare' – she was from Kilfearagh, beyond Kilrush – 'that there's only one cure when things start goin' against you at cards: under the briar, as quick ever as you can find one.'

His head jerked up. He knew exactly what it was she was talking about: the two-rooted briar. It was common knowledge, just as the Prophecies of Colmcille were, among the old people. The only bother was ... Yes, he also knew the drawback!

'What's that you're saying?' he mouthed. 'I hope I didn't hear you right. The two-rooted briar! Is it so you want to bring the Devil into this house? My father warned me many a time about the same thing. I'll have nothing to do with it, so I won't, no matter what misfortune is down on me now.'

'An' what about the misfortune that's down on me, watching you thrown there like an oul' sick calf?'

She rose, her fingers twitching. He knew better than to tempt her in such a mood and merely hung his head while she began a tirade: 'Well I knew the first day I came to this side o' the county that I was falling in with a crowd of weaklings. I could smell it off o' the place! But take my word for it, if you don't go under the briar I'll do it myself. I'll even go out an' play the cards for you, if it comes to that. Then you'll see what your so-called friends an' neighbours think o' you. If they're only avoiding you now, you'll find 'em a lot worse then. You might as well put on this skirt here now that I'm wearing. So come on. Shift yourself!'

With a stark choice like that facing him what was there for Martin to do – though he did it grudgingly – except to go out there and then to seek such a briar?

But as he shambled across the yard, he began to brighten. After all, it might take days, even weeks, to find one like that. But his spasm of optimism was cruelly and quickly dashed when Cáit joined him, the oil lamp rock-steady in her hand. She grasped his arm and led him firmly to the roughest corner of the Bull Field.

She halted.

'Look down there at your feet,' she commanded. He did so, but all he could see was a tangle of scrubby grass.

'What's that in front o' you?' Her tone was dangerous.

'Grass. What else?'

'Men! Big stupid babies. God gimme patience!'

She unhanded him, bent down and, by the light of the lamp, lovingly separated the weeds, as if this were her garden of nasturtiums and peonies behind the house. And sure enough, there was the briar, green and healthy, exactly where she knew it would be.

'Now. Test that, an' make sure you don't root it up, or God knows when we'll find a second one.'

He did so absently, for he was vaguely conscious that she had already arranged everything.

'You'll stay here now,' she said, 'in this very place' – emphasising the last three words – 'until the light o' the moon later on tonight. Don't stir. I'll bring out your supper to you.'

'Sure it could be raining all night. There might be no moon.'

'Look, I don't care how long it'll take. Stay here an' be ready.'

'But wouldn't I be doing as much good sitting inside in front o' the fire? This thing here isn't going to go away, is it?'

She paused, pondered a moment, then looked him squarely in the eye.

'Have I your word before God that you'll come out here an' go under it by the light o' the full moon the first chance you get?' She said it unsmiling, not seeming to notice anything odd in bringing God into these proceedings.

'Is it so you don't trust me, or what?'

'Don't mind that. Have I your word?'

'You have. You have!' he snapped, knowing that she would not be put off or sidetracked now that she had made up her mind as to how he must help himself.

His wait was not as long as it might have been. Luckily for him there was a full moon that night, though it showed itself only very briefly. Cáit was there, though, to make sure that he took advantage of it.

'Quick!' she urged as the clouds cleared. 'Now's your chance. Go on!'

And go he did, crossing himself as he squeezed under the briar – old habits die hard – and wishing aloud, 'May my luck at the cards come back again to me, an' multiply.'

Cáit nodded her approval and watched while he dragged his legs after him and out the other side.

'I hope you're satisfied now,' he said, 'because ...'

He stopped abruptly and snatched his hand from the ground as if he had been stung.

'What's wrong?' she asked, stepping closer.

No reply for a moment, then, 'Look there.'

His voice sounded distant, small.

She did so and saw what he was staring at, a deck of cards lying on the grass. She hesitated only for a second.

'Pick it up, will you, an' come on out o' this?'

He grasped it cautiously, nervously, and they started for the house, walking at first but then breaking into a nervous trot.

Safely inside, the door barred, they examined their prize more closely, not knowing quite what to expect. A deck of cards it was, certainly, and Martin fingered them very gingerly at first, but with more admiration as he felt their fine texture.

'Sit down,' ordered Cáit, unwilling to be impressed without proof that they were useful. 'Deal 'em out an' we'll see are they any good.'

That was done, and just how good they were soon became obvious. For Martin simply could not lose. It was as though he dealt himself five jokers each time. Out of twenty games Cáit won not even a single one and she was no bad player.

'Look at that!' she laughed at last. 'Didn't I tell you that things'd change if you went under the briar? Now, this is what you'll do. Go to Kilanena tomorrow night with that deck an' you'll give 'em a fair fright.'

This time he had little difficulty in obeying her. But his problem was to find partners. None of the old faithfuls was willing to play with him – or, rather, they all had partners, they regretfully explained. They were shortly to be very regretful indeed, particularly the two he had played with for all those previous years, for with the partners he was able to scrape up from the standers-by and hangers-on-to-the-counter he quickly went on a spree of winning the like of which had never before been seen. The first game was over in three deals, leaving gibes and laughter alike sitting uncomfortably with his mockers. Game after game he won, beating the best of the best and even those whose tokens were near perfect, yet, strangely, no one thought to question his use of his own deck all the time. Examine it, finger it they did, surely, but more in admiration than suspicion. And so the night passed, an amazing triumph for Martin and a topic of conversation for players and spectators alike as they fumbled their way home through the dark.

In the space of a fortnight all local opposition had been swept aside and so thoroughly demoralised that Martin and his team began to travel out, especially westward to places like Kilmaley, Kilshanny and Cahersherkin, in each of which places were nests of gamblers of such fierce repute that the players of east Clare avoided them at all costs; ever since 1839, in fact, the year of the Big Wind, when the best team that Tulla, Crusheen and O'Callaghan's Mills had ever put together to take on the men of the west came home stark naked of everything they owned except for their very cuff-links and rosary-beads – and these only at the behest of the priest of Kilshanny who acted as a referee of a sort, and was a Christian man, to boot. Such defeats live vivid in the memory in Clare for generations – centuries, if necessary – so it was with the best wishes of at least ten parishes, not the usual begrudgery, that Martin and his duo set off for Ennistymon one Saturday night in April.

They allowed no supporters to accompany them and Martin gave no reasons why. But his word was law as long as the mystery deck was his so they vanished into the gloom alone, but with the prayers and fond regards of many.

When they arrived in Ennistymon a crowd had gathered to examine what kind of fools these might be, to dare challenge what they could not possibly hope to beat. They were looked up and down for signs of any deficiencies, mental or physical, and then the jeering started in earnest.

'I hope ye brought extra drawers with ye, lads. Ye might need 'em.'

'They must think very little of ye at home, boys, to let ye loose in country like this.'

''Tisn't so bad. At least ye'll have the dark to cover yeer

backsides, an' not be frightening what cattle is in the country. Haw!'

There were more taunts, some not repeatable, but Martin only smiled, even began to whistle a little tune.

'We'll see whose backsides'll be out before this night is over,' he thought pleasantly, and smiled again.

They were led to the parish hall, the place of intended execution, and all due ceremony was observed – even a sort of pitying kindness. Their chairs were pulled back for them, the table wiped afresh, and then the privileged spectators gathered round in a tight huddle while all the rest – hundreds of them, it seemed – were kept back several feet by linesmen specially chosen by the priest. No chances were to be taken. This beating was to be a witnessed fact, not a matter of folklore or hearsay like the 1839 drubbing, though the truth of that same was doubted by no one.

That at least was the theory. The reality, alas, danced to a different tune. And the tune was a quickstep: one, two, three, end. The spectators had scarcely finished settling themselves comfortably when the whole thing was over. Three jinks. That was it – finished.

'Well, lads,' smiled Martin innocently, 'd'ye want another game? An' just to show we're not trying to take what ye have we'll give ye doubles or quits.'

Such an offer, the normal friendly gesture of a gracious winner, could not be refused, though at least one of the west Claremen cast his eyes nervously about him, his mouth twitching into what a close watcher would have taken for a smile. It was anything but. He was a player by instinct, the best kind of player, and knew by intuition what was about to come. But, surrounded by all these supporters intent on and convinced of victory, where could he go, what do? Nothing, except face death like a man, if such a thing were possible.

That death came thereafter by short, sharp stabs disguised by Martin's smile and honeyed words of encouragement: 'Tsk! No luck this time, either, boys? Yerra, don't worry a bit about it. Sure, we'll double it up again if ye want to. We're all Claremen here, eh? An' anyway, what could be more neighbourly than a friendly game o' cards?'

Not alone his opponents but many of their relatives in the crowd were by now having serious doubts, though; the losses were mounting far beyond the ability of a man's pocket alone to pay. Much more of this and cattle, daughters' dowries, maybe fields, might have to be parted with to level the score. In a deepening silence nervous glances were darted here and there more urgently, all gradually focusing on the priest. And he was very conscious of it, too. He began to finger his collar, his hand twitching. Then his handkerchief appeared and he was mopping his forehead, peeping out all the time from either end of that clammy white cloth as the cards were dealt one last time. He prayed then for his poor parishioners, for he felt sure that Martin would exact a revenge to match the shame inflicted in 1839.

And his prayers were answered … in a sort of way. Not in the winning of the final vital game, though. There was no hope of that, for Martin had already won two parts and was sweeping through the third as though he were faced with no opposition at all. No, the answer came in Martin's response when the men of the west were his abject, humiliated slaves, cringeing before the horrors they were sure must come.

He stood, crackled his knuckles and stretched himself.

'Well, now, this was as fine a night's entertainment as I had for a long time, an' the three of us are thankful to ye for it.'

He looked around slowly, taking in every one of all those west Clare faces. Expectation was written large in all of them: what would he do next?

'But' – and he snapped the deck into his inside pocket – 'enough o' the serious stuff. We can worry about business some other time. First of all, a drink for everyone here. Go on! We'll meet ye in the pub in a few minutes.'

A stunned pause, then a cheer almost rose the rafters. This was an offer not to be refused now that they began to try to loosen their tongues from cracked lips.

In the stampede for the door, Martin plucked the priest's sleeve and beckoned him aside. And the losers, too, of course. They all stared at him, even his own partners. He came straight to the point.

'Men, Father, I have all the figures put together here in my head. 'Twas a thing I was always good at, the figures.'

He paused, to allow this to sink in, knowing they would make the worst of the case. That he was correct their faces showed all too clearly.

'Will I tell ye now what the tally is?'

No response.

'I'll take it that that means yes.'

Another pause while he eyed them coolly, separately.

''Tis two hundred an' forty pounds, even. An' that's a fair pile o' money with a big crowd o' witnesses – including yourself, Father.'

A feeble licking of lips by the men of the west, a whitening of knuckles.

'But if I was to say here an' now, men, that I don't want to see any one o' ye out on the road, not to mind causing worry to wives an' children, would ye believe me?'

He looked them up and down. No reply.

'Ye wouldn't, from the look on ye. But that's the way it is. I have too much time spent in misfortune myself to want to bring it on any other man. So all I want is this – an' let you be the judge, Father, of whether 'tis fair or not – that ye'll pay for

21

two drinks each for everyone outside in the pub, an' give us £16 a man, the three of us, to just to cover our trouble in coming here, an' we'll call it quits. What about that?' And he held out his hand.

It hovered there a moment while they gawked at him, then at each other, unbelieving. Was this the feared revenge? They had expected to lose their farms, their very shirts. Then the priest reacted for all three. He grasped Martin's hand in both of his, pumped it violently, and was joined at once by the others.

'By the Lord, but you'll have your wish. What you ask will be done. This minute. Wait here. Don't stir!'

He pulled his team into a corner. A few moments of violent gestures and mutterings later he emerged all smiles with a fistful of crumpled banknotes.

'First of all, here's £50. Divide that three ways between ye, an' keep the £2 that's left over.'

'No, no! A bargain is a bargain, Father.'

He rummaged and brought out two well-worn pound notes.

'I'll tell you what. You keep this £2 – our donation to the church fund. Isn't that right, boys?'

His partners stood dumb, then nodded vigorously.

'Oh – ah – yes. Yes, o' course. O' course! Our offering to the church. That's it, indeed. An' welcome, too.'

The priest seemed genuinely touched.

'Well, that's ... that's a very generous thought. An' I'll remember ye in my masses for it.'

Martin, before more could be added, rubbed his hands briskly.

'All right, so! Everything is settled. Come on out then, an' we'll have a few jars. No sense in keeping the customers waiting. Let you hold on to enough money, Father, to pay the man o' the pub. I wouldn't trust myself not to run away with it,' and he laughed. They all laughed, in fact, at his little joke.

The rest of that night passed in a haze of singing, drinking and general good cheer. The only man, in fact, who refused the fourth and all following pints was Martin. He preferred to watch, surveying his handiwork – well, well pleased with what he had achieved, though as of yet how much that really was apparent to no one but himself.

But in the days that followed, as news of that night's extraordinary work spread, so also did Martin's fame – as a noble and generous winner as well as an outstanding gambler.

'By God, the man that'd do the like o' that, when he had 'em stuck to the wall, he's no everyday man.'

'Yerra, 'tis little you know. He must be a complete gom, with no sense at all. That's what has this country the way it is, fellows who can't finish what they start.'

'Can't finish? Can't? Will you have a small splink o' sense? He knows *where* to finish – which is more than I can say for some o' the politicians that's in the government at the minute.'

'Look, leave politics out o' this. Things are bad enough without bringing down that subject – unless 'tis a slap in the gob you're looking for.'

And there was many an argument, and some blows, but Martin and the reputation of his deck rose high above such piddling details, as did the good name of his parish. When people spoke now of Ballinruan there was a new respect in their voices.

'Who'd ever have thought it? There must be more than bog an' rocks there after all.'

A little trickle of curious persons even began to pay the place a visit, the first tourists ever to be seen there.

But Martin's thoughts were elsewhere. Now that the great injury of the past had been avenged and present fame at home assured, what more was to be achieved? A plague of gamblers from Kerry, Galway and Tipperary was more and more becoming a nuisance, and routinely being sent off, their tails between their legs. The team was constantly being pestered by invitations to distant places which a few months before might as well have been on the Dark Continent – Muine Beag, Nobber, Randalstown, Ballydehob, Kilmuckridge, Youghalarra. A few they accepted for the sake of being sociable, but since the result was always the same, and predictable beforehand, Martin soon grew bored. His country and countrymen began to assume for him a sameness, a staleness, that was deadening. Often he dreamt of seeing the big world outside but only once did he lay bare his desires to Cáit, on a summer's evening when the last of the sun's rays hung sparkling gold on Doon Lough.

'Aren't we kind o' stupid, to be sitting here looking at the same oul' places, summer an' winter, when we could be out exploring the high roads o' the four continents?'

Cáit looked at him idly.

'What's wrong with you now? Are your bowels at you again? I'll get a bottle from the doctor for you tomorrow.'

He sighed wearily. Had that woman no sense of adventure in her, at all? How could she bear it, to sit here drooling before the same fire, doing the same old round of chores day in, day out, particularly now that money was no longer a worry? She would not even consider a servant-girl, though he had tried time out of mind to persuade her.

'Are you trying to make out I'm a cripple, that I can't keep my own house in order? Is that it?'

He mentioned the matter no more, only took longer and longer walks by himself, turning over and about in his mind not whether he should go without her, but when. And to where.

But the manner of his going was quite different than he had

intended. The sequence of events began harmlessly enough, too, in a house in Beagh which he was visiting, invited there to talk about old times before he became prosperous, and to teach some young fellows the refinements of the Old Game. An ordinary enough night it should have been, and would have, except for some sneering comments made by one of those present, one who had been at the receiving end of Martin's luck and had never forgotten, nor had the wit to see that everyone else who played Martin was in the same position.

The comments need not be repeated. They were of the usual abusive kind – slurs on breeding and family, dark hints first of cheating, then of some unholy pact with the Devil – ramblings of that kind, which everyone else present dismissed with the contempt they deserved. The man, in fact, was laughed out of the house, booed and whistled on his way.

But within half an hour he was back, the new curate of the place in tow.

'There he is, Father. Do your duty, now.'

And that young priest was not loath to be called on. For he had come lately from a shiny new training in Maynooth, full of confidence and big Latin phrases, seeing a world full of sex, sin and seething temptations which it was his bounden duty to fight, and conquer by the grace of God. And here now was his first test, the Devil's work for all to see, for was not gambling in each and every one of its forms, and the playing of cards in particular, expressly frowned on by the Good Book and all Holy Writ?

There would be an end to this work of darkness. Now.

He stalked in, uninvited, blackthorn in his grasp, freckled country face all importance, head held severe over his new collar in the way his old Master of Discipline had taught.

All eyes were on him, though no one moved, when he spoke.

25

'So you're the man they call Martin the Cards, hah?'

Martin did not much like his tone. He took a few moments before trusting himself to answer. When he did his voice was quiet.

'My name is Martin Clune, Father, an' who "they" are I can't say. But if "they" want to call me even Martin the Pope that's fine with me.'

A titter of laughter did the rounds, only to die as the priest swung about, glaring balefully in a most practised manner.

'Silence! Let no one in this place mistake me. I'm here to do the Lord's work. An' I will, without fear or favour!'

He faced Martin.

'Show me out that ... that deck I'm hearing so much about. I want to see it this instant.'

'Sure, if that's all that's worrying you, Father, worry no more,' and Martin drew the cards slowly from his pocket, where he had plunged them instinctively moments before on the priest's entry.

'Bring them here!'

If the young cleric had had a little more experience of the world he would have known when enough was enough, but his new power, the thrill of being meekly obeyed by men twice and thrice his age was his undoing.

Martin barely stirred.

'I said I want them here. Into my hand!'

Martin could not help but smile.

'Easy, now, Father. Don't be getting all excited about a thing o' nothing. There they are. You can see 'em' – extending them in his open palm. 'But they're my own property, I'm afraid. No one else's except maybe Cáit's. So, sorry. I can't give 'em to you. Unless you want to play a game, o' course.'

He could not help adding this last little dig to his otherwise sober and mannerly answer. He should not have done it

– he knew even as he said it – but the pompous, assured face of the boy-man was one provocation too much. And anyway, was he not doing the silly lad a favour, saving him from worse mistakes, maybe?

The priest was anything but amused.

'What? You insulting vagabond!'

He raised his stick threateningly. Martin stared at him, raised his forefinger and said very quietly: 'If you want to shame your cloth, Father, do so. But I won't be here to help you to do it,' and he made to brush past him to the door. The priest's arm barred his way. His authority in the parish was gone if he backed down now.

'I want that deck!' He measured every word.

'I'm sorry, Father, but so do I,' and he flung the black sleeve from him and strode past.

'I'll put horns growing out o' your head!' screeched the young man, his voice breaking in anger. 'I'll put grass growing up to your door.'

Martin stopped, turned and smiled.

'If that's the way 'tis with you, why don't you come to the house tomorrow an' do something useful – put grass growing below in my lower field where I'm trying to grow it for the last two years. Then maybe we'll talk again about the deck.' And he disappeared into the night.

A bout of giggling rose again in the kitchen. The priest's face turned red, then purple. His mouth began to work, his teeth to grind, but only incoherent sounds came forth.

'I'll ... I'll ... nngh!'

With one last glare about him and a snort, he was gone, also into the dark.

It was not his last word, though. The following Sunday he preached a brimstone sermon at Mass, promising hell-fire and the tortures of the lost to all who aided or abetted such villainy, and by then, too, letters had reached Martin's parish priest and the bishop of the diocese, explaining in graphic detail the insult to his own dignity, the bishop's and that of the whole universal Church.

'Well, well! All of that in the big city of Beagh!' laughed the bishop, who was himself not at all averse to a game of cards. The parish priest, however, a reformed gambler and considerably more inclined to severity in his outlook, took a different view.

'This is the kind of attention the parish can well do without,' he scowled. 'But I'll put a stop to this before it goes any farther.'

Why he had not done so earlier was a question he never even bothered to ask himself, for whatever reason.

He summoned Martin to meet him in the sacristy after Mass next morning, a Saturday. Martin arrived as requested, but without the deck – he had hidden that where even Cáit would not find it, in a tobacco-tin under a flat stone in the garden.

The priest was curt when Martin appeared in the midst of his disrobing.

'Sit!'

He did not even turn, only continued his business as if Martin were invisible. Let him sweat a while. Shorter for both of us that way, he thought.

At last he faced about.

'I have little enough to say to you, Mr Clune, but you know well why I called you here, don't you?'

Oh-oh! Martin was seldom called 'Mr Clune'. He knew it boded nothing good.

'No, Father, I don't.' Better a pretence of innocence for as long as possible.

The priest stared hard at him.

'I won't waste words. I have a lot to do this day besides standing here talking foolery. You have a deck of cards. And I want it. It must be burned, and the sooner the better – before you burn instead!'

His tone was flat, final. Argument there would be none. Martin looked at him mildly, listened, but answered not a word. The priest glared.

'The Devil has his claws sunk in you. Ready to carry you with him. Don't you know that?'

'I don't know it, Father. But o' course I have only small training in theology or things like that.'

'You'd do well to remember those words,' the priest cut in. 'But no more talk! The deck!' and he extended his open hand, very deliberately. Martin shrugged.

'I haven't it with me.'

'Where is it? I want it. Now!'

''Tis at home.'

'Get it. This minute! Bring it to the presbytery.'

There was an ugly look in his eye as he said it. Without a word more Martin turned and as he closed the door softly the priest added: 'And don't stay long about it. I'll be waiting.'

It was in a blur that his next several decisions were made – or, rather, seemed to make themselves. Cáit saw him briefly, tried to talk to him. It was no use. He made straight for the garden, muttering fiercely, reappeared, hands muddy, brushed her aside, then was off on his strong old donkey-cart, whipping the animal hard. But in the direction of Tulla? Or Limerick? She sighed, shook her head. What had happened she had no notion, but when the parish priest arrived in the yard a little over an hour later and rattled a series of questions at her she let slip nothing. The clergy were all right in their own way, but sometimes ... sometimes ...

She sat at the hearth when she had the house to herself

again. Nothing to do but wait, as she had been doing so much of late. And wait she did. And wait. But without complaint now. She knew that trouble was afoot and that he would contact her when he could.

It was almost two weeks before he did so. The postman – a most infrequent visitor – arrived, a letter from far-off England in his fist, and Cáit could see that it was breaking his heart to part with it. It had been well pawed too and it seemed that several attempts had been made to peep into it, uncover what news it contained. There was little enough to uncover, in truth, a few lines only, in Martin's schoolboy hand:

Dear Cáit,

I am safe here. I will stay for a while and play cards if they lets me. I won't go hungry, one way or the other. I'll send money as soon as I can. If I can.

Martin.

That was all. No address. No good wish for herself. No ... Oh, but what of it! Let him send, or come, or do what he liked. What difference could it make to her since he would do just that anyway?

As to the writing and the money, he was as good as his word. Letters began to arrive regularly, and cash was soon replaced by bank-drafts. He was becoming sophisticated. Cáit pieced together, bit by bit, a picture of his progress across the water, and impressive it certainly seemed. If he could be believed, that is.

'I'm playing here in this workmen's club for the last week or two, and what little they have I'm carrying it from them. But when I buys pints for them all after it they forgets what they lost.'

And later,

> 'I have a leg-up got this week. This gentleman was passing and saw me
> playing. He took me to a kind of a hotel where there's tables with green
> cloth up on them. We're playing there since. The game is called bridge,
> the same as you'd cross the river with. Isn't it a strange world, too.'

And,

> 'They were saying that no one could be as lucky as me. There must be
> something bad behind it, they said. They went to throw me out, only
> that this stranger stopped 'em. He said to me private that he'd like to be
> my agent. That's what he called it, just like the landlord's man. I'll tell
> you more when I know it.'

And so it went on. And what stood out clearly was that he had
become something of a social attraction in London, for that
was where his sharp agent had taken him – 'He says we might
as well be in the middle of it, where all the big boys with the
money is.'

Those 'big boys', if they insisted on meeting Martin more
than a few times, kept only a very poor grip on that same
money, but the more of them that lost, the more there were
to take their places; wastrel sons of landed gentry, professional
men attempting to ape their social betters, dour old members
of high-sounding clubs and societies with nothing better to
do with their time all tried and all failed to get the better of
this alarming peasant from the wilds of Ballinruan – 'somewhere upstream of the Zambezi Falls, I do believe, old chap'.

Martin played his cards, ignored the insults and left the
business side of his affairs to the agent who, in spite of taking
a 50% commission for himself, turned out to be moderately
clever – he had attended a Jesuit school – and invested in

property, to their mutual benefit. Soon they owned between them a sizeable chunk of most desirable and fashionable real estate, enough for several families to retire on in splendour.

A day came at last when the agent said: 'Martin, we have enough. I don't know whether you want to keep going until you have the whole of London in your pocket. If you do, that's your business. But me, I'm retiring. And I'm doing it this very day.'

'D'you know what?' replied Martin. 'I was just thinking the same thing myself. There's no bit o' pleasure left at all in taking money off o' this shower of eejits. Too much of it they have for their own good. I'd like to see a bit more o' the world. I wonder what's things like over beyond in France.'

'Well, if that's all that's worrying you, I can point out to you a place where they think gambling is a religion. Oh, the French are an odd people when it comes to the cards. They'd even sell their wives and children, some of them, for a bet on a dice or a hand of cards.'

'They're the type o' people I want to sit down with,' Martin laughed. 'Tell me where that place is.'

'Monte Carlo is the name, and you're no true gambler, not even a well-travelled man, until your fortune is made or lost in Monte Carlo. That's what the French say anyway, whatever truth is in it.'

'Tis a thing I'll have to find out for myself, an' I'll do it before too long,' vowed Martin.

'You might be safer not to rush into anything too quickly,' said his friend. 'Look, I have the address here of a reliable man, one that'll show you the ropes there. He'll do you no bad service. Only tell him I sent you. You won't be much the worse for it.'

'But haven't I my deck? What more help do I want?'

'That might be good enough in a place where you can understand what the people around you are saying. But be sure of one thing! The French won't talk any language but their own, even if they could. The man I'm sending you to, he can talk it as well as themselves, so he'll be able to catch them out if they start any trickery.'

Martin could hardly argue with a case put so convincingly and they parted, his friend's letter of introduction safely in his inner pocket next to the cards.

The first Cáit knew of his new venture was when the postman came again, letter in hand, looking considerably puzzled. It was the stamp that had caught his attention and the lingering traces of a fragrance which Martin had added for the sheer devilment of it, knowing that noses all along the way, as well as fingers and eyes, thirsted for such little mysterious details. If it came from France, after all, it must smell good, even if it were utterly rotten, and Martin was not one to deprive people of their expectations.

Letter followed sweet-smelling letter and Cáit, between visits to the Bank of Ireland in Ennis to change francs into pounds, was made aware of the details of progress in his new haunts: how he was now playing poker, blackjack and stud, not to mention others game which had even stranger names. She was only mildly interested.

'Far more in his line to be here at home where there's spuds to be sat an' the house to be thatched. Am I expected to do everything myself?' she complained.

Like so many country people of her type it never occurred to her to spend any of the money on anything that might bring a little comfort into her life. Better to leave it safe in the bank 'for the rainy day'. Little did she realise that the bank manager enjoyed many a sunshine holiday out of such 'rainy days'.

Martin was by now far removed from considerations so

petty. His sheer skill and confidence with the cards, as well as his unfailing luck, had begun to attract the attention of others besides his victims. From being a cause célèbre in far-off Monte Carlo he took a large step up in the world when he was summoned to Paris, to grace the private apartments on Rue des Croupiers in Montparnasse. Grace them he did, too, though at some cost to their owners – who, in truth, re-mained their owners for but a short time once Martin got into his stride. It was the story of his stay in London all over again, only this time he was far more careful in the matter of his agent, the helpful Frenchman. 20% he was paid, and de-lighted to get it. And so the francs rolled in in quantities too great to be counted by any one person. Three secretaries were hired for that job alone and they worked twelve-hour days, through winter and summer alike, until their finger-tips were worn shiny from the task.

Then one night a man dressed extra-soberly invited him-self into the game at the casino where Martin was established and was by now a tourist-attraction. Before long it was obvi-ous that here was no empty-headed nobleman, nouveau-riche businessman or disguised bishop on an occasional secret spree. His play was cautious. He passed the deal as often as he let himself be included. But above all, he kept Martin fixed in an iron-grey stare. Hour after hour they sat, yet he never once seemed to tire of observing this Irishman who could not lose.

In the small hours, when all normal count of time had been discarded, Martin was about to deal yet again from behind a small mountain of banknotes when a sober-suited arm beck-oned him to cease.

'Enough, m'sieur. I 'ave seen enough. The stories I 'ave heard were not lies. So much is now clear to me. Perhaps – no? – we may speak a little in private, eh?' and he snapped his fingers. At once the proprietor was at his side, a smile back to his ears.

'Your wish, Excellency?'

'A room where we may converse. Us two only.'

'Of course. Yes. At once, Excellency,' and he bowed to a discreet-looking alcove, curtained and apart.

In the little apartment beyond, two bottles of wine stood on a round table, one red, one white. The sober gentleman bowed Martin in, towards a chair, then sat too. He stared hard at Martin, then began.

'M'sieur, in all of my days I 'ave not ... ever ... seen what I 'ave witnessed zis night. You play cards like ... like ze Devil 'imself. Which is why I must speak with you now. You see, I 'ave been sent by M'sieur le President. Your name 'as come to 'is notice. It gives 'im much pleasure that you come from ze land of 'is forefathers.'

'Wait a minute, now! Hold on. Don't say another word.'

Martin was as amazed at this latest turn of events as any man late of Ballinruan and now at the heart of France might well be.

'What d'you mean? From Ireland, is it? What's his name?'

'Ze Maréchal MacMahon. Who else?! But now, come. Let us go!'

His Excellency was not about to be denied, whatever it was that was agitating him.

'Many crucial decisions await our words zis very night!'

Martin sighed and drooped. He was beginning to be re-signed to whatever might befall him. So much had happened in so short a time that meeting the President of the Third Republic was just another incident in a now-crowded life. No more than that. He allowed himself to be hustled out to a waiting cab.

'Ze money will be safe, m'sieur, never fear. It will be deliv-ered to your 'otel without delay. Only come now. Ze President awaits.'

'Yerra, what use have I for it? Won't there be more where that came from tomorrow night? Give it to the poor people o' the town, like a good man,' and he scattered a fist of banknotes at the feet of two cringeing beggars, who were still gaping at them, stunned, even as the carriage clattered round the street-corner and was gone.

HIS MEETING WITH THE old Marshal was cordial, though cool at first. It was obvious enough that the great man had seen better days. He squinted half-blindly, his hands shook and his breath came in rasps and gasps. Even when County Clare was mentioned as the land of his ancestors he showed only a flutter of polite interest. In fact, Martin, the formal salutes done, was turning to go, pleased enough with the honour merely of having been received, when he was poked roughly from behind. Before he could turn a voice snarled in his ear.

'Mon Dieu, crétin, ze deck! Show 'im ze deck or zis visit 'as been for nothing!'

At once he tugged the cards from the pocket where he had been fingering them nervously, then presented them in his outstretched palm and smiled his most Irish smile, three teeth missing.

'Maybe ... ah ... you'd like a game, boss,' were the first words that stumbled off his tongue.

Looks of dismay creased the faces of those who understood what it was he had said, especially since all games of chance had been strictly forbidden by the presidential physician. But the story was quite otherwise in the case of the tottering Marshal. His bleary old eyes, as soon as they came to rest on the deck, took on a new sparkle. His back straightened. His heels clicked together. A smile lit up the seamed old face.

'Sacré bleu, mes amis! At last, ze possibilité of a game! Let us test our wits with real strategy and throw from us zis ... zis death-in-life, zis formalité.'

With a sudden energy electrifying to those who knew him from his military heyday he ... not quite leaped, but lurched to Martin's side and hustled him to a nearby table. The attendants were already there, settling chairs, smoothing a green baize cloth into place.

And so they played – poker – seven different permutations of it. For the remnants of that night and until dawn was stretching itself into the full light of day. Martin won of course, as inevitably he must, but the Marshal proved himself a wily opponent, certainly not the geriatric relic he appeared, and the more public money he lost the younger he seemed to become, until by the time that game at last broke up he was all for settling down into a drinking-session at some bistro – the seedier the better – though he had already consumed well over two bottles of brandy in the course of the night.

His attendants were frantic with worry, but even more astonished.

"Ow can zis be? Where does ze energy come to 'im from?'

But in spite of all their dread they were delighted too, particularly his physician, who had been applying leeches to the old man for some considerable time without any noticeable effects except fits of shivering and weakness.

As they were parting, therefore, it was not entirely surprising that Martin should receive an invitation to return. And thus a pattern was begun: for three days every week thereafter the President became incommunicado. It mattered not what business of state called, which invited imperial delegation kicked its heels at the gates or what important piece of social legislation awaited the Presidential thumb-print; nothing could be done until after the thrice-weekly poker-game. And the old Marshal was definitely getting younger. Of that there was no doubt. All the signs and symptoms were there to prove it. From being a semi-invalid he had progressed to early morning strolls, then to brisk trots. Now he was leading his young officers a merry dance each day – and doing the same, if not more, with fashionable ladies at night, only some of whom were unmarried. Something urgent must be done, it was decided, to preserve the dignité of the Presidential office, the gravitas, the illness proper to the age of its occupant.

But with Martin to hand that was not possible. He must be cast off. For the good of France. The Marshal was severely told so – and at once demonstrated some of his old fire by promoting Martin to the Cabinet without so much as a word of consultation with his advisers. One day a gambler; a responsible member of Cabinet the next, his new title (in a position designed especially for him): Créateur de Bonne Humeur.

In any English-speaking nation this would have been laughed to scorn, but not in France, land of imagination, culture, esprit. And the results were soon apparent. Negotiating-sessions, whether at the Board of Commerce or at the Ministry of Foreign Affairs, became much more business-like when word got about that the reward for brisk service was a place at the Presidential poker-table. Even those diplomats and civil-servants who had not the slightest interest in poker could not, for their careers' sake, let slip such an offer, and so, for the first time in almost a decade (since the Franco-Prussian war, in fact) the country began to assume a definite direction, as if steady hands had at last been laid on the tiller of state.

Further honours followed: with much ceremony Martin was made Chevalier of the Empire as his Christmas present for 1878 – a rather empty honour, since there was no longer much empire to speak of except in darkest Africa and parts of Asia that were difficult to pronounce, let alone find. Yet it was the thought that mattered, and Martin graciously accepted whatever came his way.

And so it continued. No matter what government was in

charge thereafter – and they were mainly of a Republican hue – he was present with his Devil's prayerbook to keep each one on course. And when the old Marshal finally relinquished power in January of 1879 he disappeared at once without trace; the gambling members of the Cabinet had almost to be forced to attend his sad handing-over ceremony, since the games were now a seven-day-a-week matter.

Under the guidance of Jules Ferry the new government seemed fair set to cast off these evil habits, but the good intentions lasted less than a month, and within a year there were worse troubles – the religious turmoil caused by Jules Ferry's foibles saw to that – and all because of a mere six nights' consecutive losses to Martin's deck.

'The same Jules was ever a bad loser,' was Martin's verdict. 'But to take it out on religion, an' to put the good men an' women o' the religious orders walking the roads o' the world! I never thought he was that low.'

Year followed year in a glow of prosperity for the man from Ballinruan – carriages, properties, even two personal servants – yet in spite of his enormous prestige and vast, ever-growing wealth, he remained a countryman at heart, charitable to a fault and still easily shocked, though by now he had been seeing government from its rotten inner core for well nigh twenty years. The Dreyfus Affair of 1894 proved one such distasteful upset; it was almost the cause of his throwing up all he had accumulated in the City of Light.

'If we had a man the like o' him in Ireland 'tis promoting him we'd be, instead o' persecuting him,' he wrote to his wife. Her reply was short and to the point: 'Just like we did to Parnell, hah?'

No more was said on this matter, nor about returning home, either.

And time passed away, old age tightening its squeeze until

a day came, just as Europe was flexing its muscles for another great effort to destroy itself, when he felt that his death was upon him. This time he knew it was pointless to call on the services of his doctor, but, kind as ever, he allowed that worthy to twitter and fooster about him; to do less would, he knew, be to wound professional pride.

The services of a priest he did demand, however. But when the abbé came and Martin explained, in the course of his confession, how matters stood, the holy man shook his head gravely.

'It grieves me to tell you, m'sieur, that I cannot give you safe passage to ze Other Side until zat deck is in my possession. Destroyed it must be.'

Martin's face fell. It had been a reliable friend when human hearts and hands had been ranged against him. He could hardly betray it, even now.

'That's Cáit's property – she's my wife, Father – as much as 'tis mine, an' I can't part with it without her permission.'

'In zat case,' and he shrugged regretfully, 'I can do nothing.'

He rose to go.

'Tomorow I shall return. Perhaps your mind may change, eh? Think deeply on ze consequences, my friend. Ze Devil, a hard master he is. Beware of 'im. Repent, and fling zese filthy cards from you while yet zere is time.'

He paused at the door, but continued on out with a sigh and a shrug when Martin showed no sign of flinging anything.

'He'll come back. There's no fear o' that. I never yet knew a priest not to come back to where there was money.'

But this was France, not Ireland. The abbé did not return. His footsteps died away and Martin was left to his own thoughts in the silence of the gathering night. It was one of the longest he ever spent, and lonely, too. His servant – Ballinruan native thrift had never allowed any more than one to be on duty at any given time, and sometimes, as now, there was no one at all – would not be back on duty until seven o'clock in the morning. Till then he was alone. Or should have been.

One o'clock sounded. Half-past one. Two. Memories crowded in, both happy and sad, keeping him from sleep. He tossed painfully, this way and that, tried his best to rest, but there was no comfort to be had. Tired, bleary-eyed, he heard four o'clock strike, yawned heavily, then ... caught the scent of something that should not be there. It was the smell of smoke! Fright gripped him. To be burned in bed – that was no fit end for a man of means. He levered himself out on the floor, groaning, then fumbled to strike a light. But before even a spark was lit: 'Hhumph!'

A throaty voice rumbled in the darkness. Martin nearly wet himself with the fright of it. A thief in the room? A murderer? But before he could even disentangle his thoughts the voice came again, this time in words, slowly, evenly.

'Don't mind the light, Martin. There'll be plenty o' that where you're going – an' heat to go with it.'

Martin froze. He had placed it now, the voice, and only too well. The Old Lad was here, punctually, for his part of the bargain of the briar. Whose else could it be? For a few seconds there was no sound except the thumping of Martin's heart. Then the Devil snapped his fingers and the room was filled with an eerie glow, enough to make younger blood than Martin's run cold, especially since the dull flame flickered from the Dark One's thumb, which he held out before him.

Martin stared, and icicles of fear stabbed at his insides; there was nothing at all of feeling on the swarthy face, in the brooding eyes that held him fixed.

'Time up at last, Martin. I hope you enjoyed yourself.'

He said it lazily, then stepped forward, wrenched open the locked press where the cards were kept now in a golden box, like relics in a shrine. Not the slightest respect did he show to this, only snapped off the lock as if it were a piece of straw. He yanked back the lid and there the cards lay on a satin cushion, worn but still very serviceable. For an instant Martin thought he was going to suggest they play a game, but no. All he did was reach in, grip them gently and sigh.

'Welcome back, children. And thank you for another safe delivery.'

He pushed the deck lovingly into an inside pocket and for the first time smiled.

'There'll be more customers for that, I don't doubt!'

Then closing a fiery grip on Martin's arm he propelled him from the room.

'Come. Time for us to hit the road, eh?'

There was no point at all in arguing. Any court of law, in this world or the next, would uphold his claim to Martin. It was better to go with a quiet dignity if not a good grace.

When the servant came on duty at 7 a.m. a smell of burning greeted her. She rushed upstairs, to find the bedroom door wide open, the bedclothes thrown back, but no other sign of violence or disorder.

'Seigneur! Seigneur! Où êtes-vous?'

She might as well have been calling the wind for all the reply she got. And when the police were summoned the mystery naturally deepened since they were anxious to conceal their bafflement by propounding deep theories. Anarchists, obviously, must be responsible – communards, or other enemies of the state – particularly since several safes where Martin kept his cash were found open, their doors hanging askew. Each one smelt strongly of burning and the charred remnants of much paper were found within. The police, even their experts, hard-bitten men who had witnessed every crime conceivable to the imagination, were left scratching their heads.

Only the abbé, when he was allowed climb the stairs and

enter the room towards evening, seemed not in the least surprised. But his opinions he kept closely to himself. What he knew would not sit well with modern scientific police methods, so there was no point in mentioning it. He merely fingered his beads as he made his dejected exit, knowing too well that another soul had slipped through the Divine Net.

The furore in the newspapers – 'Rapt! Enlèvement! Meurtre!' – lasted a week or so, then sank out of sight as it was replaced by some fresher sensation.

And the golden box? As soon as it was finished with as evidence it was returned to Cáit in Ballinruan, under RIC escort. Naturally, such visitors caused much interest and many questions, though none of them directly to Cáit. And she, for her part, chose to make her neighbours none the wiser, though a few of them did catch a glimpse of the box.

But a few days after the visit she was observed entering a bank in Ennis, a large, obviously heavy, package in her arms. And when she emerged back on to the street her hands were seen to be empty.

Maybe this is why it was whispered at the time, and is still rumoured today, that that same box rests in a steel safe in a vault at Bank Place, Ennis, unopened, unclaimed after all these years.

But that may be no more than hearsay. For everyone knows how quickly each little grain of fact becomes festooned and decorated with rumour in that part of Ireland. Yet, how stubbornly it has resisted the years ... and grown ever more certain with the passing of time.

Strange, indeed ... Truly odd.

Larry and the Devil

There's a saying in Ireland: 'God is good, but the Devil isn't bad, either – if you know him!' There lies the bother, of course: getting to know him in a way that's safe.

Larry Hartigan lived with his wife Sara in County Limerick, in the parish of Athlacca, and even though his neighbours looked on him as a strong farmer, Sara was stronger. Part of her strength came, without doubt, from her hatred of all drink stronger than milk – which was unfortunate, because Larry liked nothing better than a skite with his friends now and again, especially one where there were heady brews to lend energy and fire to the songs and dancing of the assembled Gaels.

At that time, at funerals, weddings and all other outings, there was sure to be drink a-plenty, whatever else. It was cheap, and the people liked it. For that reason all such gatherings were sorely looked forward to; they were among the few reasons poor people had for carrying on in the drudgery of daily living. Athlacca was no different to anywhere else in that regard. All that was needed was the hint of an excuse; a death in the parish was as good an excuse as any.

Old Mick Fogarty died. It was as simple as that. Larry, as well as every other able-bodied person of sound mind in the parish, would have to present himself at the wake-house on at least one night out of the customary three. That was the least that might be expected. It would hardly be decent not to appear and send a few prayers after the soul of their neighbour, after all.

But when he was going out the door of his kitchen that night, Sara's last words to him were: 'Listen, you! Be warned. Don't touch a drop. An' be home early. Say your prayers an' come out of it, like a good man.'

He said he would, but promises are one thing, the keeping of those promises another thing entirely, especially when pressure and temptation are applied to do the opposite – as they soon were to Larry. For when he walked in the door of the wake-house, the first thing that was put into his paw was a crock of poitín. No wake would be correct or complete without plenty of the same stuff; maybe that's the reason why the priests hated the very sight of it!

He dithered for a second or two, remembering Sara's words, but he was too fond of it to resist for long.

'It'd be bad manners not to take it,' he said to himself, 'an', sure, one won't do me no harm, anyway.'

But one led to two ... three ... four, and so the night slipped on. Those present were in a serious, subdued mood, naturally enough, and Larry didn't feel he could just up and walk out. So he stayed, joined in the spirit of the proceedings and drank as much as he was offered.

But some time during the night – or, more correctly, in the early hours of the morning – a little thought wormed its way up from the depths of his befuddled mind, and that thought was of Sara at home, sitting up waiting for him. He stirred himself.

'Oh! Oh, I must be going,' he croaked, and tried to make his way to the door. Unfortunately, in that place where there was only one door when he came in earlier there were four doors now, all of them dancing and jumping as if they were doing a polka. He blinked stupidly, swayed and nearly fell. Lucky for him there was a woman nearby who was more sober than he was. She caught him just before he went into a spin and put him sitting on his chair again.

'Begor, Larry,' said she, 'you're looking a small bit shook. Sit down quiet there now an' say your prayers, an' you'll be all right. What's your hurry, anyhow?'

'In the name o' God, let me go!' he croaked. 'I must get home or I'll never hear the end of it.'

He struggled up again in spite of her and started for one of the four doors he could still see dancing where there should be one only. He made a drunken man's choice: the wrong one. His forehead collided with the wall and he collapsed in a flurry of whitewash-flakes.

'God help us all this night, but poor Larry is takin' oul' Mick's death fierce hard, entirely,' said one man crouched by the fire, sucking his dúidín.

'He is. He is,' nodded a companion. 'Fierce to the wide world, isn't it, what a bit o' grief'll bring a man to.'

After three or four attempts to get out, someone came to the conclusion that something other than grief was blinding Larry's eyes. He found himself being picked up by strong hands, dusted off and steered outside.

'Hi, Larry,' said a voice that seemed a long way off, 'I'd go home the shortest way if I was you. 'Tisn't safe to be out this time o' the night any more with the blackguards that's in it now.'

With many good wishes the door was closed behind him and he was left in the darkness, alone except for the rustling of unknown busy couples in the bushes around. He looked here and there vacantly out of bleary eyes and saw nothing for a few minutes. Then the limewashed piers of the gate gathered themselves out of the haze and beckoned him to start his journey there.

He stumbled towards them, almost fell, but made it at last after several half-circles and many steps sideways and backwards. He threw his arms round one of them and held on for dear life.

'Saints preserve me this night,' he gurgled, 'but if I don't go home soon she'll kill me.' He had still sense enough left to realise that. He began to debate with himself whether he should take the road or go by the fields, but that was the poorly attended debate and one that was quickly over: 'I better go the shortest way, whatever else.'

He started out from the safety of his pier the best way he knew how – on his hands and knees – and crawled along the road, taking both sides, until he came to the stile he was looking for. Now, at last, he felt safer. Home was only a few fields away. Unfortunately, that was where the drink betrayed him one more time. He was no more than halfway across the first field when he realised, from the slope of the ground, that he was going in the wrong direction. Yet, no landmark showed itself and as he veered this way and that he began to regret that he had left the road; however long it might have been it would at least eventually have led him to his own door.

A clammy sweat insisted on gathering itself on his back and he could feel it trickling into the depths of his trousers. It was an uncomfortable sensation. Desperately he tried to pull his wits together, but they would have none of it. They were bent on going their own way, and did so now with a vengeance. Larry flopped down and almost cried. But the thought of Sara of the fierce welcomes soon set his legs in motion again and eventually, by keeping close to the hedge, he found the next stile. By repeating the same process in that field he came, at length, on the third opening. But the night was moving on, and at the rate he was progressing it would be morning at least before he laid eyes on his house. Sara was even now probably making delicate preparations to receive him!

In that third field he stumbled suddenly to a halt. There before him, flowing silently, was the stream which bounded his own farm. Glassy-eyed, he stared at it.

'Well, blast it,' he mouthed petulantly. 'How did I forget about this? An' how am I going to cross it?' – for there was no bridge, only a narrow beam of timber. He continued to stare stupidly, then, with the confidence of drink whispering, 'Go on! Try it,' in his ear, he gathered himself and laid his left foot gingerly on the plank. It held firm. Smiling, he put the other foot in front of the first. Still safe and sound. His courage growing with every step, he was making noble progress when, near mid-way across, disaster struck. For whatever reason he faltered, stopped, and once he was no longer moving a fit of the staggers came on him. Instantly the plank turned over and down went Larry with a roar and a splash. And so it was that he had his first bath in six months.

He shot up like a tomcat out of cold water, and made for the opposite bank, spluttering and shaking water from himself. He dragged himself out, very sober now, and stood shivering, looking down at the stream, poison in his eyes.

'May the devil take me if I ever come this way again,' he spat and turned miserably for home, hugging himself for warmth.

Sara must have heard him squelching into the yard, for when he arrived at the back door, looking like a drowned rat, she was waiting. Straight away she lit into him and preached him a fiery sermon that soon dried him out.

'You latchico! You useless gamall! Walking the roads of Ireland full up o' drink at all hours when you should be at home in your own house minding your defenceless wife. What kind of a man are you, at all? Or are you a man?'

A lot more was said in that same vein to Larry that night, and he was the quiet boyo that crept into bed just as dawn was breaking, with his solemn oath given to Sara that he would stay off the drink not just for evermore, but for ever and a day.

She kept a watchful eye on him for the next several weeks,

and it seemed as if he might actually have learned manners, for not a drop of anything stronger than tea or spring water crossed his lips in all that time.

But sometimes things go wrong in spite of all good intentions. The neighbours in that parish had no consideration for Larry's problem. They would insist on dying, and at most inappropriate times, too. A short time after his warning from Sara another of them started out on the long road to eternity.

Larry was in a bother. 'Look here,' he said to Sara. 'I'll have to put in a bit of an appearance at the wake. I'll be shamed if I don't turn up. An' so will you!'

What could she do but agree?

'All right,' she said in her quietest, most threatening tones. 'You can go. But if you turn up like you did the last time, you'll sleep out with the dog beyond on the flagstone for the next month, hail, rain or moonshine. I'm warning you, stay away from the drink, that's all.'

'Have no doubts in your mind about that, a chroí,' he said. 'I won't touch a drop.'

He meant it, too, and moreover he kept his word, because it wasn't one drop he drank at all on that outing but several. He was ever a truthful man, Larry! But in the middle of all the merriment, in the dark hours of the night, the same thought as before came to him: the vision of Sara waiting for him at home. All the fun left him of a sudden and he struggled for the door. This time he found it himself, staggered to the gate-piers and measured up in his mind which way he should go: by the road or by the fields. Something told him to take the long way round by the road, but the fear in him advised him to go by the short-cut. It was the fear he obeyed, as before – and the same meanderings that held him hour after confused hour in the self-same three fields after that. It was just before dawn when he came, exhausted, to the same stream of water at his own land. The foot-plank was still there, never stirred since his last visit. He hardly noticed it. Or if he did he was damned if he would trust it after the low trick it had played on him that last visit.

He stepped back three paces, straightened up, aimed himself, then ran, intending to leap the water at one go. Mo léir! He came short of being the champion he thought himself, as many a drunken person has. He landed with a splash and a screech in the middle of the pool. But when he tried to drag himself out on the opposite side he found his way blocked by a huge shadow, one that blotted out the very light of the moon. He stopped dead. There was no sound from the creature looming over him. But though he was too frightened to speak he moved quickly enough, against the stream, and tried to clamber out farther up. But again the dark shadow stood before him and there, even in that cold water, he felt a chill of a different kind entirely and the last dregs of his drunkenness drained from him with alarming quickness. He turned back towards the near side of the stream but had moved no more than two steps when a low voice growled from the depths of the tall shadow: 'Stop, Larry! Don't stir one other inch, except in this direction. Come here! We have talking to do, the two of us.'

There was nothing for Larry to do except turn and face whatever it was that commanded him so fiercely. He blinked and replied in a faint voice: 'Who are you, sir, an' what d'you want with me? I'm only a poor man, if 'tis money you're after, an' all I want to do is go home in peace to my bed, 'cos 'tis little peace I'll have when I get there.'

He was almost crying.

There came what sounded like a guffaw from the dark silhouette – only there was an edge to it that was far from humorous. Then a deep voice rumbled: 'Larry, do you remember the words you spoke last time you came this way?'

There was silence, as Larry searched in the depths of his memory and then an even more ominous pause as one by one those words of his came back to him. There was no escaping them, try as he might to do so.

'Do you remember?' demanded the voice, shocking him from his silent struggle. He replied slowly, reluctantly, and as he did so the full, terrible meaning of what he had promised began to trickle like an icy sweat along his skin. In a flash he knew who it was that was speaking to him, but before he could do more than twitch with fright a strong hand grasped his arm and a voice hissed in his ear: 'Come on with me now, like a good man, quietly an' according to your own words, an' there'll be no trouble. We have a long journey to travel this night, you an' me.'

Larry felt hot fingers burning their mark into him and for a certainty he knew who it was that spoke. No use now to be regretting his rash words of that previous journey – 'the Devil take me if ever I come this way again'. The time was here; the Old One had arrived, and unless Larry could think fast and clearly all was lost. But devil a thought came to him as he was dragged along, further and further, step by step away from his own familiar fields.

For a long while not a word was spoken; the Devil kept his own counsel, and Larry was too busy coming to terms with this new and unwanted development. But at last, in the midst of wild, unfamiliar surroundings and as they approached the dark entrance of what looked like a cave he realised that if he remained silent any longer there would be no coming back. A desperate idea leaped to him, out of he knew not where, the tip of a lifeline of hope, maybe.

'They tell me, big man, that you're a powerful lad. Is that true?'

The Devil paused.

'They, whoever they are, know nothing at all about me. But 'tis true, anyway.'

Modesty about his own achievements was never one of his virtues.

'Oh, I can well believe it,' said Larry in a sugary voice, 'because they told me too that you can do anything you like.'

'Indeed I can,' smiled the Devil, and Larry noticed that he showed no inclination to move on into the cave. 'An' what else did they tell you about me?'

'Oh, that you were better than any druid that ever lived at changing your shape when you wanted to.'

The dark man seemed pleased.

'I don't know who your friends are, Larry, but I'd like to meet 'em sometime. They know a lot about me. An' 'tis true. I can change myself, all right. Any time I want.'

'Oh, would you ever do it for me, please, before you take me into that horrible place there beyond, where there'll be no light to see you?'

'Well ... I don't know have we time for that now ...'

'Yerra, go on! What'll it take only a couple o' minutes? An' I won't ask you for anything else ever more.'

The Devil fingered his nose, rubbed his fingers thoughtfully, then snapped into a smile.

'All right, so. Just this once. Tell me, what'll I change myself into?'

'Ammm ... could you make yourself ... as big as an oak tree?'

'Why wouldn't I?' snorted the Devil. 'Simplicity itself!' And he began to breathe and breathe in, sucking up huge gusts of air, almost swallowing Larry in the process. He swelled out like a balloon, larger and larger, until finally he was blotting out the light of the moon for the second time that night. Larry clapped his hands to his eyes, pretending fright.

'Oh, I believe you! I believe you!' he squealed. 'Be careful, will you, an' don't fall down on me.'

The Devil let out an evil chuckle of triumph and slowly released the air in a long ugly hiss. When he was back to his own size he reached for Larry's arm once more.

'Now,' he boomed, 'you have your proof, so we'll be going. Come with me.'

'Hold on one second, now,' cried Larry, pulling his hand away. 'I'm just after thinking of something.'

''Tis a bit late for thinking now, my boy. You'll have no need of that where I'm taking you.'

'But 'tis important,' begged Larry.

'Make it quick,' snapped the Devil, 'because we're expected down below about now!'

'Well, 'tis this. Maybe you're not as powerful as you'd like poor innocent people like myself to believe, hah!'

The Devil glared at him, a poisonous dart.

'What d'you mean? How dare you –'

'Hold you on there, now, my man.' Larry was fully sober now and going nowhere without a struggle. And he saw that he had rattled the big fellow. 'Sure, doesn't everything grow up? What you did there was nothing great at all. Couldn't I do that myself if I had as much time to practise as you.'

The Devil seemed baffled for an instant.

'What're you trying to say?' he rasped. 'That I have no power? Is that it?'

'No! Not at all,' smiled Larry. 'I'm only telling you that I'd be more inclined to believe you if you could grow down as well as up. But can you do it? That's the big question.'

There was triumph in his voice.

'Grow down, is it? You miserable weed. That's no problem to someone like me.'

'You're all talk, big man, but I don't see you doing it. Make yourself the size of – ah – a cat.'

The Devil snorted in disdain, blew out a mighty blast of foul air and began to shrink and shrivel before Larry's eyes.

'Hmmm! Not bad,' murmured Larry when the change of size was complete. 'But you'll have to do a small bit more before I'll believe you once an' for all. Can you make yourself as small as a grasshopper?'

'Not just as small as one, stupid man. I can turn myself into one. Watch this!'

Larry put on his most impressed look as the Devil did just as he had promised.

'Well? D'you believe me now?' came the tiny voice from below.

Larry's first urge was to stamp on him there and then and be finished with it, but out of respect for grasshoppers he only said, in a mild voice: 'Kind of. There's one last thing I'll have to see you doing before you'll convert me.'

'What is it?'

The little voice was ratty now.

'Could you jump into this?' – slipping off his old-fashioned purse from round his neck and opening the thong which tied its mouth, all in the one movement. He placed it on the ground inches from where the grasshopper crouched.

'That wouldn't be hard,' sneered the small voice.

'Do it, so,' returned Larry. 'I'll believe you when I see it.'

Whether the Devil saw the danger or not, his pride was stung and with a single bound he landed in the farthest-back, darkest corner of the purse. But if he did, Larry was on it in a flash. His hands grasped the thong and the mouth of the purse snapped shut, trapping the Devil inside. Larry gleefully wrapped the thong three times round the neck of the pouch, slipped a miraculous medal on to it, tied three tight knots in it and held it up.

'Aha, boyo! I have you safe now, an' 'tis there you'll stay many's the long day.'

There was a short pause, then the Devil let out a string of the most horrible and vicious curses ever heard in the land of Ireland. Smoke and a smell of brimstone oozed from between Larry's fingers, but he held on grimly to the purse as he made his way towards home, realising full well that there was nothing but it and the medal between him and a very hot future indeed.

So far so good, but he had no clear notion of what to do with the cursed article now that he had it in his power. Odd thoughts came to him: 'Why not give it to Sara an' see whether the Devil can put up with her for long?' or 'Maybe I should take it to the church an' put him swimming in the holy water font an' see how he likes it.'

It was no such notions that solved his problem, however, but a stranger thing entirely; he was no more than halfway home when he heard the clash of hurleys and the fierce yells of sportsmen in a field nearby. He stood, amazed, for who could be playing a match at that hour of night? Yet the noise continued, coming ever closer, if anything. Still clutching the purse, and for dear life now, he crept forward to where the hedge gave way to a low stone wall. He crouched, peered through the gloom and, sure enough, saw the game in progress no more than a hundred feet away. He watched, hardly daring to breathe, as those two teams of fierce battlers rushed here and there, sweeping the sliotar before them, first to one end of the field, then back to the other. Larry, a great fan of hurling, sank down on to the wall, fascinated by their skill and toughness. He winced as seasoned ash cracked and thudded against heads, shins and ribs, but no matter what injury they received or how heavily those men crashed to the ground they always seemed to leap up as quickly as they had been stretched.

'Bedad, but aren't they the hardy lads?' whispered Larry to himself, the Devil all but forgotten in the excitement of the fray.

Over and back, up and down the play flowed, a score at one end answered a moment later by another at the opposite posts. No mercy was shown, no quarter asked for. It was for all the world, Larry decided, like a meeting of the men of Kilkenny and Tipperary, the best of neighbourly ferocity.

All thoughts of home, the Devil and the world around him vanished as he settled into the swing of the game, perched as comfortably as the stones allowed, and many a time he had to clap his hand to his mouth to stop himself cheering as this or that player struck a shot more skilful than any before.

But then, disaster! One of the biggest men on the field snatched the sliotar out of the air, stampeded up the pitch with it, yelling and brushing men – friend and foe alike – aside like flies. Only once did he pause, just outside the square, and that to take aim. Then, as the goalkeeper cringed in a corner of the net, he released a murderous shot. Larry could hear the whistle of it as it bulleted home. He bit his nails, waited for the goalie's death-screech, as did every man present. Instead, there came a loud crack as the ball hit the crossbar and glanced over, off into a field a mile away, a field, moreover, which was thickly overgrown with furze and briars. The bar collapsed in two neat halves, and it was this that broke the spell.

From every side they rushed to where the scorer stood and began to glare at him and then abuse him.

'Didn't we warn you not to blast the ball like that?'

'You half-eejit, you! What're we going to play with now, hah? We have no spare sliotar. Didn't you know that as well as any of us, you oul' ape, you?'

A torrent of the most foul abuse cascaded down on the poor man's head. He cringed and apologised feebly, but the damage was done. The game was finished, ruined, unless the ball could be found, and quickly.

'Get out there – now! – an' find it. Don't come back without it or ... or we'll finish this match with your head,' roared the captain of his own team. And he slunk away, the backs of his hands dragging along the ground as he went.

'That's all very fine to say,' growled the opposing leader, 'but are we going to have to stand here whistling to ourselves for the rest o' the night while that eejit is tying to find it?!'

'Don't mind looking at me, you gamall,' snarled that worthy. 'It wasn't me that did it.'

'Who d'you think you're calling a gamall, fathead? Is it a feed o' teeth you're looking for?'

Tempers were rising dangerously, and Larry saw by the way the men began to close ranks behind their captains, gripping their hurleys short as they did so, that in no long time a full-scale faction-fight would be in swing.

Without thinking of the possible consequences he rose from his resting-place and shouted: 'Stop, men! Don't ruin as fine a game as ever I saw by fighting now. Here, look' – and he held up the purse – 'I have a ball here that'll do ye until the other one is got.'

There was a shocked silence, but before a word could be said he flung in the purse and the nearest man to him caught it, as by second nature.

'Here, gimme a look at that!' snapped one of the captains, all the time keeping Larry in his sights.

He squinted closely at it.

'Bedad, it isn't the regulation weight, but the size is all right. What d'you think of it?' he said, tossing it to the other captain for inspection.

'It'll do. Elegant. Anything that we wouldn't have to replay this game.'

'Throw it in, so, will you, an' we'll play on.'

No sooner said than done, and without another glance or word for Larry the teams were at it again, more fiercely than before now that every man had got back his wind. Hither and thither they thundered and the clash of their hurleys rang and rebounded off the surrounding hills. Larry was delighted at this new display, and all the more so when he considered what they must be doing to the Devil inside the purse.

In truth, they beat the living stuffing out of him, and though he yelled for mercy his screams were drowned out by the roars and battle-cries of both teams. What bones were in him were broken, and no one but himself and Larry any the wiser. They might have crippled him entirely, only that well into the second half the large oaf in the field of furze jumped up suddenly, the real sliotar in his paw.

'I have it at last!' he yelled and lumbered back to the pitch like a big child with a new toy.

The game shuddered to a halt and one of the captains strode to where Larry sat, the purse a limp, squashed thing in his hand.

'Stranger,' he said, 'here's your ball back. A bit the worse for wear, I know, but you'll excuse us for that. We're thankful to you for saving our game. But go home now, an' on your life tell no one you saw us here tonight. If you do ...'

He said no more, but the way he glanced at the purse told Larry all he needed to know. He was in no doubt that that was how he too would look if he failed to keep their secret.

'My lips are sealed, sir. You can depend on me. An' ... an' ... I'd just like to say I'm proud to have been able to help ye. The like of ye isn't in Ireland for the hurling.'

The captain gave no sign that he had even heard the compliment, only turned on his heel and walked away to where his men were waiting. Larry did likewise and when he paused a moment later to get a last glimpse of them he found himself staring at an empty field with never a person in it, living or otherwise.

Fright began to prod at him then, but he was consoled somewhat to feel the purse crumpled between his fingers and hear low broken groans from within. He made no more delay, only hurried to his own house – where he found another problem awaiting his attention. For there, hands on hips, stood none other than Sara, armed with that most lethal of weapons, her tongue. She meant business; that much was clear. But Larry surprised even himself when he marched past her, in the door, swinging the purse and humming a little tune, as if she were invisible. She was dumbfounded. Not a single threat, not even a word could she muster; just stood there paralysed and foolish as he sauntered into the kitchen and skipped lightly on to the chair nearest the dresser. With a flick of his wrist he threw open the lid of the box on top of the dresser where they kept their few valuables – American letters, rent receipts and such like. Sara's eyes never left him as he threw in the purse and snapped the lid closed.

'Now,' he beamed, 'where's my supper? I have a fierce hunger on me from all the praying I did at that wake.'

He pulled in the chair to the table and sat waiting, whistling a little tune all the while.

Still shaken, not believing what she was hearing and seeing, Sara meekly went about preparing the food, though throwing suspicious glances now at Larry, now at the box.

But even when he had eaten enough and was smoking his pipe at the hearth afterwards, never an attempt at explanation did he make in spite of all her pointed looks. At last he stretched himself and knocked the ash from the pipe.

'Time for the bed, I s'pose,' and he yawned, and began to climb the stairs. Sara could bear it no longer.

'Hi! Are you going to tell me what's that thing you brought in, or not?'

He paused, but did not turn.

'Time enough you'll know about it,' he said quietly, then continued on his way.

She followed close on his heels, still questioning, but getting no answers. They went to bed, but even when Larry at last turned towards the wall and began to shake the rafters with his snores there came no peace to Sara. Try as she might she could not sleep. Instead, she tossed and turned, her mind wrestling with the mystery. Finally she could bear it no more.

'I must know what's in that box – an' I will!'

She got out of bed, padded downstairs, and without even pausing to light the lamp, climbed on to the chair and pried up the lid of the box. She rooted around inside until her fingers touched on what she was searching for. With a little squeal of satisfaction she lifted it out and carried it to the hearth. There, in the dim glow of the dying embers, she tried to open it. But Larry's three knots had, if anything, been made more secure by the battering on the hurling-field.

'I won't let it beat me, whatever else,' she muttered, crossed to the dresser and returned with the carving knife. That made short work of the thong.

Her thumbs scrabbled to tear open the mouth of the purse, but though it gaped darkly no gold tumbled out. Or silver. Or coppers. Nothing. She shook it, mystified.

'If this is his idea of a joke, I'll ...'

She was interrupted by a hissing noise from that small patch of blackness, followed by a terrible smell, as of something long dead and rotten. Then a head popped out, but the features were of no person who had ever walked this earth.

The eyes were bloated and almost closed. A large gap was where teeth should be. Every inch of skin was torn, lacerated or covered in welts and bruises.

Sara screamed and would have flung the purse from her as though it were a live coal. But the Devil was faster. He leaped bodily from his prison, head-butted Sara between the eyes and streaked towards the door.

All at once the kitchen was filled with a clamour of noises: the chair clattering, Sara falling, shrieking and clutching her head, the Devil hissing, and then, above it all, an ear-splintering crash as he struck the front door and carried it and the jambs before him in matchwood out into the yard, then galloped into the night, raising sparks from the ground as he went.

Tired as he was, Larry shot up in the bed in the room overhead, landed his two feet on the floor and scrambled towards the stairs, thinking there must surely be robbers in the house. Three steps short of the kitchen floor he stopped and stared dumbly at the scene of confusion before him – his wife stretched, moaning, in the ashes, her chair upended, the front door gone. He could hardly take it all in.

Then he saw the purse, cast aside on the floor! His lower lip dropped foolishly and he clapped his palms to his ears.

'Oh, no!' he moaned. 'Don't tell me you ...'

He rushed towards the object, horror in his face.

'Don't tell me you let him out, you óinseach.'

If Sara was shocked by his reaction, she quickly enough recovered her wits and snarled: 'What óinseach are you calling me, you bastún!'

She rose up before him, threateningly, despite her late injuries.

'An' why didn't you bother telling me what was inside that cursed purse? Is it so you wanted me to get killed? You never tell me anything in this house. I'm sick an' tired o' you, so I am.'

Larry hardly heard her. He knelt, picked up the purse and examined it, rocking himself backward and forward, fear in every line of his face.

'Oh! Oh! Oh!' he sobbed. 'Why did you do it? Why couldn't you leave him where he was? I had him safe an' you went an' destroyed it all. Women!' – and he spat out the words bitterly – 'They'll always be interfering, whatever else.'

'Oh? Is that so, indeed? An' what about the men of Ireland, as useless a set of gobdaws as ever wore socks? Who are you to be giving out oul' guff about women?'

The argument started in earnest then, and who got the best or worst of it concerns no one outside that kitchen. What concerns every one of us, though, is that a rare opportunity of keeping the Old One in his place was lost that night. But the sad fact remains: he escaped, even more vicious than before his tangle with Larry, and is out there in the big world ever since, lurking and waiting, as the catechism tells us, 'for the ruin and damnation of souls'.

The terrible pity is that he need not be.

Jack o' the Lantern

EVERYONE HAS HEARD OF Jack o' the Lantern, surely. But how many people know how he came to have that odd name?

It all started in County Clare, in a little place called Cratloe. A man named Jack McCarthy lived there one time, but no one called him by that name. He was known far and wide as Jack Murt, and the same man was the friendliest person in all that side of the country. He'd talk to anyone, anytime. And to do that he had to be meeting people, and what better way of doing so than by being out at night in every rambling-house in the district, for there were no better such houses in all of Ireland than there were in east Clare in those days. So good was the entertainment to be had in them that it was nothing strange for crowds to be heard laughing their way home across the land at three and four o'clock in the morning most nights of the week.

One particular night Jack Murt was out as usual, chortling his way past the graveyard in Sixmilebridge, remembering a specially cutting reply old Willie MacMahon had sprung on Jamesy Curran at the end of a most involved tale of family character-assassination. It had almost caused a battle, and would certainly have ended in bloodshed had not the woman of the house taken a hand in the proceedings by taking down her rosary-beads and ordering all present to follow her in a few prayers 'for all them gone before us'. This tactic succeeded in calming tempers, for by the time that all the 'trimmings' were said most of those present had quite forgotten what the excitement was about in the first place. The prayers and a final cup o' tea 'for the road' had ended the outing on a relatively happy note, and here was Jack now, in the dead hours of the night, breaking into a whistle to keep himself company as he picked his steps in the moonlight, for the roads were in a deplorable state, and more than one of his acquaintances had turned an ankle on such a journey as this.

As always when passing a graveyard gate, he blessed himself and nodded a little prayer in the direction of the departed. And then he saw it! The shape of a man, standing with his back to the left-hand gate-pier. Jack stopped, drew in a breath sharply and then bowed a stiff little bow.

'God save you,' he managed. 'An' how are you?'

No reply from the figure.

Jack squinted at him again.

'Are you all right, or is there something I can do for you?'

Still no reply.

'Yerra, blast him,' muttered Jack to himself then, 'if he don't want to talk let him scratch himself off o' the pier till morning,' and he walked on with one last salute over his shoulder as he went: 'Good night to you, whoever you are. An' take my word for it, you'd want to have a share more talk or you won't go far in this world – or in the next, either.'

Little did he realise what it was he was saying. He was gone only three paces when he felt two hands grip his shoulders, wheel him around, and he found himself looking into a yellow face.

He was so shocked that he could do nothing for a moment, not even speak. But the man spoke, in a low hollow voice with an edge of excitement to it.

'I'm two hundred an' sixty-seven years, three months an' fifteen nights with my back against that cold pier, an' you're the first person in all that time, the first one' – his voice cracked with emotion – 'that ever spoke to me three times. There's a few of 'em that saluted me. An' a drunk man on a September night – I'll never forget it – spoke to me the second time, but you're the only one that ever said the third word to me. An' because o' that I'm free. An' you're going to be rewarded.'

Jack stared at him, amazed.

'Yerra, what reward? I want no reward. Isn't that why we got mouths – to talk to people? What reward would I want for saying a few words to a stranger?'

He was scratching his head now, genuinely surprised, but the man held up a warning finger.

'Never mind that kind o' talk! You're going to get three wishes, an' you're going to get 'em now.'

Jack shrugged his shoulders.

'All right. I won't be arguing with you here at this time o' the night, but what in God's name would I wish for? Haven't we everything we want, myself an' Máire – she's my wife, you know.'

'Wish!' snapped the man. 'You must take your wishes when they're there.' Jack saw that he was dead serious, and rather than be disagreeable, which went against his nature anyway, he said: 'Ammm ... ah ... well, we have all we need at home, like I said' – and then he brightened – 'except furniture. We have nothing much in that line except a couple o' stools an' a few forms – as well as my oul' rocking-chair by the fire, the only comfortable piece o' seating in the house. But that same chair is purely cursed. An' why? 'Cos as soon as anyone comes into the kitchen that's the seat they'll always make for. D'you know something? I'm hardly ever able to sit in it myself. Someone is always there, warming it, an' I'm sick an' tired of 'em all. So, all I'm asking you now – just for a bit of a joke, you know – is that the next person to put their backside in that chair won't be able to stir out of it until I give my permission. Will you grant me that?'

The man looked at him.

'That's the talk of someone with little sense,' he said, 'but you have it. Now, make your second wish.'

If Jack had had trouble with the first wish, this was even worse. He hummed and hawed, whispered and muttered to himself, but could come up with nothing. The stranger began to get impatient.

'Hurry on!' he snapped. 'I can't wait here all night. I want to go home to my nice warm grave. It'll be the first night I rested comfortable in it since I was brought here two hundred an' sixty-seven years, three months an' fifteen nights ago.'

The preciseness with which he repeated the numbers would have been a warning to another person, but not to Jack.

'Don't rush me. I'm not used to thinking at this hour o' the night.'

Then a glimmer of hope. The garden!

'Hold on! I'm after remembering something. Out in our garden at home there's an apple tree, an' a mighty tree for fruit, too, until the young blackguards o' the place found out about it an' started coming in over the wall to carry every apple that was ever on it. Myself and Máire, we didn't get an apple off o' that tree for the last five years, so we didn't, an' 'tis high time a stop was put to 'em. Will you ever grant that the next person that puts a hand on the fruit o' that tree will stick to it an' won't be able to move from there until he gets permission from me.'

The man looked coldly at Jack.

'By the Lord,' he said, 'that's another wish from a man without too much between his ears. But you have it. Now, there's only one wish left, an' my advice to you is use it more wisely than those other two.'

Jack stood and thought, then plumbed the depths of his empty mind once more, but though he scratched his head, his palms and his backside, he could come up with nothing.

The stranger began to lose patience with him in all serious-
ness.

'Come on, will you!' he snarled. 'It'll soon be morning an' I
have to be back in there' – jabbing his thumb towards the gateway – 'before the light of day.'

Still no ideas from Jack. The man stepped closer, his nos-
trils twitching.

'Didn't you tell me you have a wife at home? If you can't
think of anything for yourself, maybe she'd like something.'

Jack beamed.

'The very thing! A hard-working woman she is, too, the
same Máire. An' she has this bag that she puts all kinds o' little
bits an' pieces o' material into, collecting 'em up to make quilts
an' covers out of 'em. The only bother is that every time the
cats come in around the house, the first place they make for
is that bag, to make their load in it. Many's the time the poor
woman put her hand into something soft an' ugly inside in
the same bag. You couldn't teach manners to cats that are
dirty by breeding, you know, so can I ask you now that the
next thing that'll go into that bag won't be able to come out
of it until I'll allow it? That way I'll make 'em suffer even if I
can't change 'em.'

The man threw up his eyes to heaven, wondering, no doubt,
what kind of an amadán he was dealing with, but he replied
evenly enough.

'You have it. An' much good may it do you.'

With that, he vanished like a wisp of smoke between the
bars of the graveyard gate and Jack saw him no more. There
was nothing for him to do except go home, go to bed and
sleep soundly. Which he did, too tired out to give a further
thought to the strange thing that had happened him.

But all was not well, for first thing when he got up the
following morning Máire confronted him with, 'There isn't a

splinter o' timber there for the fire. Go out, will you, an' cut a few sticks?' So he went up with a hatchet to the fairy-fort in the High Field behind the house and began to chop down one of the whitethorn bushes growing there. And all this in spite of the fact that it was a place his father and grandfather had always, from his earliest years, told him to keep away from: 'Don't have nothing to do with it. Keep out from the Good People an' they won't interfere with you. Anyone who has close dealings with the same crowd isn't the better for it.'

Yet, here he was now on this morning, doing exactly the opposite. Obviously something had gone seriously wrong with his head.

But he had barely landed the fourth stroke when a sliver of wood flew and struck between his thumb and forefinger – a most sensitive spot. He dropped the hatchet and tried first to pinch it, then to suck it out. But with no success. And since he could not continue working he hurried down to the house, called Máire and told her his bother: 'Look, I'm after cutting my hand. Get a needle, will you, an' try to pick out that bit o' timber. 'Tis paining me.'

She tried, but even though she was a skilful woman at such things she could not come at it. In fact, all she seemed to do was drive it deeper and deeper until it was up almost as far as his elbow. She had to give over at last and by then Jack was so far gone with pain that he had no option but to take to the bed.

By the following morning the hand was swelled horribly. When evening came it was the size of a football. And by the morning after it had gone black. Altogether a most ugly combination.

Máire did not like the look of it one bit.

'I'm in dread that you'll lose that hand,' she said, and all Jack could do was toss, turn and moan. He became delirious, and each day thereafter saw him worse than on the day before. He gave Máire no sleep or peace, but the only relief she could offer him was bucket after bucket of cold water from the well. In it she kept his hand and arm immersed, hoping and praying for a small miracle.

'Sssssss!' would go the steam out of the bucket as soon as hand and water met and shortly the bubbles would begin to rise, and so another bucket was needed, until Máire was worn out from the constant carrying.

For five days this went on. The doctor was brought then but could do nothing since Jack would not allow the hand to be amputated.

'Sorry for your trouble, ma'am,' said he as he left, pocketing his fee, 'but I can do no more.'

The priest fared no better, and at last all was despaired of.

On the evening of that fifth day Máire was sitting at the foot of the sick-bed, sobbing quietly, when she heard a loud, firm knock. She looked up, half dazed from exhaustion and grief, then staggered to the door and opened it. Standing there was a tall swarthy man, his coat flecked with dust as if he had travelled many miles.

'There's a sick man in this house, isn't there?'

He spoke in a deep voice. Máire started.

'How did you know that?'

'I smelt it miles back,' he grinned, but without any trace of humour. 'Now, woman, take me to his bedside. Talking here like this isn't helping any of us.'

'W-who are you, an' why are you here?' she stammered, but he paid no attention, only pushed past her, flung open the door of the sick-room and took one level look at the man on the bed.

'Ah,' he sighed, still grinning. 'He's gone. Finished.' And there was something like satisfaction in his voice.

Máire was about to cry out when he added suddenly, 'Finished, unless ... unless ...'

She stared, then whispered, 'Unless what, sir?'

'That's for me an' him to talk about,' he replied grimly. 'Go out, woman, an' make a dreamall o' tea. I'll be with you shortly.'

He showed her firmly to the room door, then closed it quietly behind her. He returned to the bed, sat close to the dying man and said: 'Jack, you're for the high jump. You know that, don't you?'

All Jack could do was nod, then with a great effort he whispered: 'Only too well I know it. I'm in fierce pain.'

'Ah! I'd well believe that. But I might have a bit o' good news for you,' smiled the visitor, 'because, you see, there *is* a cure.'

His smile grew wider as he said it.

Jack tried to struggle up on his elbows, failed, then croaked: 'Give it to me, please, sir ... for my poor wife's sake even more than my own.'

'I might do that, right enough,' beamed the stranger, and then in a more sober voice, 'but there's a price I'll have to charge. You can't expect such a cure for nothing.'

'I'll give you anything I have,' sobbed Jack. 'Anything, as long as I wouldn't die.'

The visitor arose.

'Hmmm. You'll give me anything, will you? Lucky for you, then, that I'm a reasonable person. All I want from you ... is your soul.'

The last word was like a rock falling on Jack's head. He gaped up, looked straight into the eyes that were amusedly observing his every move, and knew at once who it was that stood before him: the Old One himself, none other than the Dark Lad. The Devil. He licked his lips. Only now did he notice that they were bone-dry. But he could say nothing for the moment. His mind was racing, though: 'What'll I do? I wish herself was here to advise me. But I'll have to give him an answer … an', sure, what other answer could it be only "yes"? I don't want to go to the Other Place before I have to. I know little enough about this world, not to mind the next one.'

His heart was thumping, his hands shaking, by the time he found his voice and heard himself saying, 'All right. I'll give it to you. But I want something more than just my life for it.'Tis worth more than that to you, I'm fairly sure.'

The Devil gazed at him evenly.

'Little men on their last legs should never try to drive hard bargains. But I'm a fair person as well as reasonable. What is it that you want besides?'

'Seven years o' health, wealth an' happiness. What good would my life alone be if I couldn't enjoy what's left of it? If you can give me that much you can have my soul, an' welcome.'

The Devil pressed his fingertips lightly together, pursed his lips and allowed his gaze to wander to the ceiling. There was a brief but deep silence. Then he snapped his attention back on to Jack, startling him, and said in his most pleasant manner: 'That's the way it'll be, so. I like my … companions … to have a bit o' spirit in 'em,' and he tittered, as if he had unburdened himself of a very subtle joke, then reached down. The tip of his left forefinger touched Jack's afflicted limb and in the space of a second all that had been a throbbing, pulsing mass of pain was quieted and soothed. The affliction, the poison, was banished in the blink of an eyelid.

Jack was too astounded to attempt even a single syllable. Then, through that silence the Devil paced to the door, turned, and without the least explanation said, 'I'll be back. Seven years' time. Be ready.'

He walked out, a little smirk curling the corners of his mouth, and strode past Máire, who jumped back from the door, where she had been listening, as soon as he wrenched it open.

'D-did you do anything for him, sir? Any chance of a cure?'

He made no reply, only stalked out the front door. She leaped towards the room, and what she saw stopped her in her tracks, for there was Jack putting his two legs out onto the floor as he might on any ordinary morning, seeming to be not one bit the worse for his late illness.

She stared at his hand. It was as sound as if nothing had ever been the matter with it. She dashed back to the front door and looked up and down the road. But there was no one in sight. The road was bare and empty for as far as she could see. Amazed, she turned again and began to fire questions at Jack: 'What did the man do? Did he say any prayers? How did he ...?'

'I know no more than yourself, woman. I was so surprised at what was happening that I didn't even get a chance to ask him his name.'

He did not mention to her the bargain he had made, nor his near certainty as to the identity of the 'doctor'.

'But what of it? Haven't I my health again, an' that's all that matters.' After a little pause he added, 'An' I wouldn't be a bit surprised if our luck began to change for the better. 'Tis well coming to us.'

Máire nodded, happy to agree, for after what she had just witnessed anything seemed possible. But she was no fool, and in quiet moments began to put the facts of the case into some kind of order for herself. Also, she had heard stories of cures like this before now from the old people. And in all these tales the magic came from one of only two places ...

Yet she hoped for good times ahead and put her fears from her as best she could.

AND SO IT CAME to pass as the 'doctor' had promised; their fortunes changed. Legacies came their way from relatives they never even knew they had. England began another of its wars somewhere and the price of hay and cattle doubled as a result, and then doubled again, all in the space of weeks. A large leather purse was left on their doorstep one December night with a brief note: 'Conscience-money. I owed your father this.'

All these and more saw to it that within the year they were wealthy beyond their wildest dreams.

Their neighbours were dumbfounded, of course, but since Jack and Máire were free with what had come their way so freely, no one asked too many questions.

'What's good for one is good for all,' they nodded wisely, bending the old saying to fit the bright new circumstances.

And so the time passed, all the more quickly because it was spent so deliciously, until the seven years had gone by without Jack and Máire noticing. In fact, the awakening, when it came, was rude and sudden. They were at their dinner one day in the month of September, savouring the usual (by now) fine food, when the servant-girl – another of the additions of fortune – entered, curtsied and said: 'There's a man at the door, sir, and he says he wants to talk to you.'

'Tell him I'll be with him when I'm finished here,' growled Jack, unwilling, as always, to interrupt a meal if he could at all avoid it.

The girl went out, but was back in a moment.

'He says it can't wait, sir. He has to see you, an' now.'

Jack flung his knife and fork to the table and rose with a snarl: 'By the Lord God, he'd better have a good reason for this, whoever he is,' and stumped to the door. The sight that greeted him there stopped him dead in his tracks: it was none other than his benefactor, the 'doctor', and he was smiling out of his swarthy face. But Jack, to his credit, recovered himself instantly and without more delay held out his hand as if in welcome.

'Muise, how are you, oul' friend? You wouldn't be hungry by any chance, would you? 'Cos if you are, you're at the right place. The dinner is on the table. You must have smelt it. Come on in, an' have a bite to eat.'

Máire, drawn by the voices, hurried out, only to let a little squeak out of her when she saw who was there.

'Oh, merciful God, Jack, run! Run, or he'll carry you!'

Jack silenced her with a careless backward wave of his arm.

'Run? Indeed I won't run! Will you have sense, woman? What way would that be to welcome a guest?'

He turned again to the Old Lad.

'You're sure you won't eat a bite?'

'I am. An' what's more, I'm in a hurry. So, be coming on with me now, like a good man. We have a journey in front of us, you an' me, an' trouble or delay is the last thing any of us want, surely.'

'All right,' said Jack. 'If you're in a rush I won't be the one to hold you here.'

He beckoned to Máire. 'Make a drop o' tea for our friend here, an' I'll just go up in the room an' pack a few little bits an' pieces for the road. I'll be back shortly.'

The Devil could hardly refuse a request so innocent and padded into the kitchen, letting an approving eye roam over the warm comfortable room that he had indirectly provided. Jack stepped to the bedroom door.

'Look, big man, wouldn't you sit yourself down while you're standing? The road'll be long enough in front of us.'

The Devil glanced about, saw Jack's rocking-chair by the fire, its arm-rests shiny from years of happy fingering, and sat down without another word or thought, while Máire pottered busily about the tea-making.

Jack, meantime, was standing just inside the room door, tittering behind his fingers, his eyes dancing. Slowly, carefully, he counted to fifty, then shook himself, cleared his throat noisily, and stepped back into the kitchen.

'Well, I'm ready any time you are, big man. Are you coming, or waiting for the tea?'

The Devil smiled, swung himself forward, and tried to rise from the chair. But no matter how he pulled, growled, strained or snarled, not an inch could he raise himself. He cursed, swore, dragged a bit more, then collapsed backward, frustrated.

The next half-hour was something between frightening and funny for Jack, Máire and the servant as they watched and listened to the rising tide of vile abuse and more and more frenzied movements. Every trick the Devil knew – and they were many – was tried to shift himself from the chair, or the chair from the floor, but they failed, each and every one. His trousers were the first casualty, followed closely by hair and skin from strategic parts of his person, but no matter how close he came to escape there was always some piece or other that refused to part company with that accursed seat. And so at last he fell back, baleful, panting, exhausted.

Jack sat quiet on a three-legged stool at the other side of the hearth, a wide, sympathetic smile decorating his face. In the charged silence he leaned across, his hands dangling between his knees.

'Yerra, aren't you the foolish lad to be tiring yourself out like that, an' maybe injuring yourself, too? An' all for nothing. 'Cos you're going nowhere.'

The Devil sprang him an evil glare, then broke into another bout of frenzied tugging, teeth bared, snarling.

Jack leaned back, sighed as if weary, but secretly enjoying every iota.

'There's no teaching manners to some people, I s'pose. But whatever about that, I can tell you bad news now: you won't move one inch out o' that chair until you get permission from me.'

The Devil stopped.

'Permission? What d'you mean, *you* give *me* permission?'

From the tone of his voice it was obvious that there was something here he did not understand.

'Just what the words mean. That's all,' smiled Jack pleasantly. Then he added, 'An' I'll give no such permission until I get a little favour in return.'

The Devil must have suspected what was coming for he did not reply, merely glowered, his lips twitching.

Jack continued evenly. 'That little morsel of a favour is seven more years of wealth, health an' happiness. No more. Well, what d'you think?'

A deep silence settled on the kitchen. The servant-girl stood frozen, her mouth gaping, fish-like. Máire picked her nails nervously, as if afraid that her man had over-reached himself. But he only smiled, whistling a soft little tune.

'I'm waiting,' he crooned at last, mocking. His tone was not lost on the Devil. Curling his lip, he sucked up something greeny, ugly from the depths of his insides, then 'Pthu!' – it landed, quivering and slimy on the toe of Jack's boot, where it began to hiss and splutter.

'All right,' said Jack, watching the disgusting object intently, ready to fling off the boot should that be necessary. 'If that's the way of it, maybe you'll think again after a year or two here at the hearth on your own. C'mon, Máire. We'll move out o' here this day an' close up the place entirely. No one'll know he's in it, an' I'll bet you there isn't many a one that'll miss him, the low cabaire.'

He was speaking now as if they, both of them, were quite alone. She was only too relieved to go along with the suggestion, and turned on her heel.

'Stop! Wait!' gritted a voice through clamped teeth as they pulled the door behind them. Jack shoved his head back in, no longer smiling.

'Tell me, true this time, what is it you really want?' the lad inside hissed.

'Just what I said,' replied Jack. 'I'm not a greedy man. Only gimme seven more years o' health, wealth an' happiness for myself an' my wife here an' I'll be satisfied. That isn't much to ask now, is it, from the likes o' yourself that has all the time in the world on his hands?'

'We'll see how much when your day o' reckoning comes,' muttered the Devil grimly.

'What's that you're saying?'

'I said all right, you have it. Seven more years. Not a day more, not a day less. Just like you said yourself. Now let me out o' this.'

'Oh, you can go any time you want to,' smiled Jack. 'Don't think we're holding you at all.'

With that, the Devil rose, cautious now, fearful of doing further damage, but when he saw that he was indeed free he paused, pointed a dangerous finger at Jack and hissed, 'I'm going. But I'll be back. Oh, never fear but I'll be back. An' when I do, I'll ...'

Jack laughed towards Máire.

'Could you believe it, but he don't want to go? He must like us better than his own crowd below at home.'

Delicately, as if walking among pieces of broken glass, the Devil padded out, muttering obscenities as he went, as well as threats: 'Oh, but my turn'll come ... an' that'll be the sorry day for ye ... Never forget that!'

And he was gone.

They stood a few moments staring at each other, as if they could not believe the business finished so tamely.

'That wasn't so bad, was it?' breathed Jack. Máire could only shake her head and laugh, long and heartily.

'I never thought you had it in you to get rid o' him,' she said firmly, relief showing in every word. 'But who is he, an' what brought him back after all that time?'

Jack considered. Now might be as good a time as any to come clean.

'Sit down,' he said quietly, and then called the servant-girl.

'Make that drop o' tea, will you, an' bring it here to us?'

When that was done and she had been sent about her duties in the yard he looked his wife in the eye.

'I wouldn't tell you a lie, Máire, an' there's no use in running from the truth. 'Tis like this ...' and he explained to her quietly, simply, all that had been transacted between him and the man at the graveyard as well as the bargain he had sealed with the 'doctor' for his soul.

She listened, in a way he had never known her to do before, and when his last word faded and a clammy silence had gathered again in the room she looked across at him mournfully. 'I had a fair idea that 'twas him that was in it, the Dark Lad. There's no escaping him. You know that, don't you?'

Jack tried to look on the bright side.

'Well, there's no use having the bad word all the time. God is good, an' even if He turns the blind eye to us, we'll think o' something.'

Máire, if she was shocked by his shaky faith, did not say so, but she was noticeably silent for the rest of that day. And the next. In fact, it took a fortnight, several visits to the chapel and many lighted holy-candles before she would consent to enjoy their renewed good fortune. Even when she did so there was an extra emphasis on good deeds and charitable works, as if they might soften the blow when it came.

Jack was engaged in less spiritual chores: he bought a strong new scraps-bag – largest size – in Limerick's most fashionable store, as well as a fist of mothballs, brought it home and presented it to Máire.

'There you are, now. Empty the old one an' give it here to me.'

Mystified, she did so, and he folded it and placed it in their bedroom wardrobe, empty except for the mothballs.

After that he had one thing more to do: see to it that the old apple tree in the garden should want for no loving care that he could lavish on it. If they had had a son he could have been no more pampered than that tree was in the days, months and years that followed. In fact, the more time that passed, the closer Jack's daily routine centred on it until Máire began to feel neglected in spite of all her good works and the crowds of burly beggars and hardy supplicants that dogged her every generous step nowadays. She said so, too, in no uncertain terms. But, 'I'm doing this as much for you as for the tree, if you can believe that,' was his reply every time. Many a day she thought of cutting it down herself, or of ordering one of the many strong mendicants who infested the yard to do so, but something in Jack's manner as he tended it always made her change her mind at the last minute.

And so the months wore on, one plodding doggedly, inevitably in the tracks of the one before, until the seven years were no more.

It was September again, humid, drizzly weather, no use for working in, though comforting to look out on. And that was what Jack was doing that Saturday morning, a faraway look in his eyes, when 'Thud! Thud! Thump!' – three loud knocks sounded – on the back door this time. Jack leaped almost a foot in the air, but steadied himself. Máire, who was knitting at the table, dropped her needles and cocked her head, listening, intent.

'Ah,' sighed Jack. 'He's here. I'd know that knock anywhere. But what brings him creeping in that way, I wonder?' – nodding towards the rear of the house. 'Is it so he isn't man enough to face us straight out?'

He shuffled to the door, wrenched it open – and stepped back in mock surprise, then bowed.

'Well, well! Look who's after coming to see us, Máire. Our benefactor.' He almost sniggered at his own cleverness but caught himself. 'Come in, sir, an' don't be standing there in the rain. You could get your death.'

The Devil's eyes narrowed; a long sharp talon tapped Jack's chest.

'I won't, or come in. You caught me once before, but you won't do that again. Collect your stuff, whatever you have to bring, this minute. You're coming with me, no more about it, an' when I get you in *my* kitchen we'll see how funny you'll find it. I have special spits prepared an' pointed even now, an' plenty hands willing to turn you over a slow over a very hot fire.'

Now it was his turn to smile, but it was a hyena's grin, with nothing of humour in it.

'So come on!'

Jack threw him a disappointed glance.

'Lord, but aren't you the spiteful animal? No bit o' pleasantry in you at all.'

He turned away with a shrug.

'What of it? I was expecting as much.' He reached in under the table and brought out his travelling-bag.

'What's in that?' snapped the Devil.

'Only a few odds an' ends I might need.'

'Little you'll want – especially in the way of heavy clothes. An' don't bring your overcoat, either,' he chuckled dryly. 'The climate you're going to, you'll hardly need it.'

"Tis a help to know that much, at least,' Jack replied pleasantly, and then to Máire, 'Slán go fóill, a dhuine. I'll see you when I'll see you, I s'pose.'

There was time for no more, for the visitor clamped his hand on Jack's arm, and thus linked he was escorted off briskly round the corner of the house.

Máire rushed through the kitchen to the front door and dashed after them, pleading, 'Please, sir, please don't take him. He's all I have. What'll I do without him?'

The Devil wheeled, let out a mighty blast of breath that whipped her off her feet and rolled her helter-skelter back to the door.

Jack was impressed.

'You have no shortage o' wind, anyway.'

'If you had to start as many fires as me every day, you'd have good wind, too,' scowled the Devil. 'Now, come on. I have more time spent here than you're worth.'

Jack only smirked and walked on, leaving Máire to collect her wits as best she might. But just as they were passing out the gate he dug in his heels, and pulled the Devil back.

'Just one second,' he begged. 'Gimme a chance to take one last look at my oul' garden, will you? Many's the gallon o' sweat I poured on it, to make it what you see there now. Take a close look at it. You have nothing like it below, that's one thing sure. Am I right or wrong?'

His tone of certainty nettled the Devil, but he stopped in spite of himself for a peep.

'Look at all them rows o' gooseberry an' blackcurrant bushes there, an' not a weed to be seen. D'you think that happens by itself? 'Twas these two hands that did it,' and he held them up so that his companion might be in no doubts.

'Very nice, I'm sure, but I'm not interested. Come on! We have enough time lost.'

'One thing more, an' we'll be on our way then. Tell me, did you ever see a finer apple tree than that one there beyond in the corner, or better fruit than the stuff up there at the top of it?'

'Indeed I did,' sneered the Devil, looking closely at the tree.

'I have more experience of apple trees than you think, smart lad. Oh, I can remember a day ... high walls ... an' a fine strong woman ... her husband asleep ... That was one o' the best day's work I ever did.'

He seemed lost in happy moments, until Jack interrupted him.

'Well, if you like apples that much, wouldn't it be a friendly thing to bring a handful of 'em home to your wife an' young lads. You're welcome to 'em as far as I'm concerned, so you won't be stealing 'em if you take 'em.'

The Devil hesitated and seemed amused by this notion. Jack could see that he was interested though undecided.

'Sure, even if they don't like 'em at home, wouldn't a few of 'em keep us chewing on the journey?'

The Devil's tongue flicked his lips; his eyes lit greedily.

'All right,' he whipped. 'But stand there an' don't stir.'

'Anything you say,' shrugged Jack, all innocence, as his companion vaulted the wall and streaked across towards the tree.

'Make sure you get the ones up high. They're juicier, an' there's no dust on 'em,' Jack shouted, but the other needed no such counsel. His eye was already fixed on a cluster of shiny red fruit peeping from a collar of leaves three-quarters of the way up the tree. He stopped a few feet out, leaped at least three times his own height and snatched at them. But he got no further, neither up nor down, for as soon as ever his fingers touched them he stuck fast and no matter how violently he tried to shake himself free he could not.

Jack, his elbows resting on the wall, was observing all this with growing amusement and in a few moments Máire joined him. They watched as the Devil swung, over and back, hither and yon, a stunned silence surrounding him.

'Wouldn't he make a lovely Christmas decoration?' cackled Máire.

'I'm not so sure o' that,' murmured Jack, more cautious. 'Wait, an' watch. He's not finished yet.'

And right he was, for with a howl and a twist the Devil attempted to break the branch. But try as he might he could make no impression on it. And the angrier he became the more violent grew his squirmings, the louder his cursings. Yet the apple he was clutching would not fall. And then, in pure flusterment, he struck out with his right hand to free his left – a costly error, for in an instant that hand was as solidly stuck as the other. He saw at once what the case now was, let out a piercing shriek and began a savage dance which sent showers of leaves to the ground, but not one apple.

In the space of an hour he had exhausted himself, the tree was bare and Jack and Máire were as close to happy as someone else's misfortune had ever brought them.

'God forgive me,' said Jack, 'but wouldn't it do your heart good to see that fellow stuck up there? He suits the place better than wallpaper.'

The Devil heard him, as he had been intended to.

'Let me down out o' this, or I'll ... I'll ...'

'You're in no position to be making any threats now, boyo, so quieten your dirty tongue.'

It was sheer luxury for Jack to be able to talk yet again to the Old One like this, and he was going to draw every last bit of pleasure from it while he might.

'You're staying there for as long as I decide. Come on, Máire.' He beckoned her. 'We'll leave him to think about things for a while, an' maybe when I talk to him again – oh, in a month or two, when the fine, frosty nights are in – he might have something to tell us that we'd like to know.'

They walked away, slowly, soberly, back to the house, closed the door quietly and left the Devil hanging, foolish. But if they were expecting another outburst – as they surely were, for they hastened to park themselves inside the kitchen window – they were disappointed. Not a move from the tree. Never a sound. Only baleful, staring eyes and ... was it a hurt silence?

Their annoyance quickly began to show, and Jack would have gone back out to taunt further, but Máire, wiser, said: 'No. Leave him there a while. The less notice he gets the more he'll look for. Isn't that what the missioner used to say long ago?'

Her advice prevailed, and all that day they went about their chores without another glance towards the garden. Night gathered, and as a bedtime farewell Jack came to the door, ever kind and concerned, and called into the dark: 'Yoo-hoo, out there! D'you want anything before you settle ... ah ... down for the night?'

A low snarl answered him together with a rasping suck that Jack recognised only too well. He slammed the door, not a second too soon.

'Phlup!'

A quivering green ball of slime hit it and began its slow burning trickle to the ground, stripping the paint as it went.

'He's a low curmudgeon, an' no doubt about it,' Jack scowled. 'I'm in doubts that we'll ever teach him manners.'

'All we can do is wait an' see,' Máire added, though without much conviction. Yet oddly enough, morning showed a wholly different slant to the affair, and a side of the Devil's character that Jack would never have suspected. A bellow from the road-gate started it.

'Hi! Jack! Are you in there?'

It was Jeremiah Horan, their next-door neighbour, on his way to the creamery. But he was going nowhere at that moment, only standing by his donkey, a look of confused wonderment in his face as he stared in at the apple tree.

Jack appeared at the back gable-corner, not willing to take the front-door route again, especially by light of day. Too risky, he thought.

'I'm here,' he shouted back at Jeremiah. 'What d'you want?'

'Nothing, only to know what in the name o' Heaven is this thing here hangin' from your tree.'

Jack laughed, then frowned.

'I'm afraid that lad isn't there in the name o' Heaven, whatever else.'

'But who or what is he, at all?'

By this time several other neighbours had gathered, jabbering, pointing, all excited. Jack's courage rose with their numbers and he soon felt brave enough to join them. More and more questions, while all this time the subject of their curiosity hung there before them, silent, unmoving.

'I can tell ye very little at this time,' was all Jack would say, and since they were well acquainted with phrases like this from their County Councillors they were satisfied in a sort of grudging way. But not entirely.

'There's something odd about this whole thing,' declared a man of the O'Hallorans noted for his piety. 'I think maybe it'd be no harm to tell the parish priest about it,' and he began to hurry away.

Jack saw the Devil's jaw drop, his eyes widen.

'Aha,' he grinned, sensing a bargain waiting to be speedily struck. O'Halloran was hardly out of sight when he whispered hastily to Jeremiah: 'Look, Jerry, listen to me. 'Tis important you don't ask no questions, only do what I'll tell you, an' as quick as you can.'

Horan nodded, impressed by his friend's tone and the urgent look in his eye. 'Talk on.'

'Take away this crowd, will you? Anywhere, as long as 'tis a distance from here. An' do it this minute. Please.'

Horan shrugged his hands, a 'what can I do?' look on his face.

Jack thought fast, plunged his hand in his pocket and pulled up a cloth purse.

'Here,' he gasped, thrusting it into his friend's grasp. 'What's in this'll buy pints galore for 'em, an' anyone else ye meet along the road too. An' have a few yourself. Go on, quick, before I change my mind. They'll follow anyone anywhere when drink is mentioned.'

How right he was was instantly proved when Jeremiah came to life, tossed the purse in the air and cried, 'Well, well, boys! A sight the like o' this, 'twould give a man a thirst, what? Come on! Down to the pub, quick. I'm buying the drinks, whatever ye're having. Double if 'tis whiskey.'

Dumbfounded though they all were – for neither he nor anyone else had funds enough to be standing rounds of drink out of the blue like this – they raised a ragged whoop of delight and asked no questions. A man's word was his bond; the offer had been made. How it was to be paid for was none of their concern.

They scuttled off in a happy cluster, all except Jack.

'I'll join ye in a while, maybe. I have a few small bits an' pieces to do here around first. But ye could do something for me.'

'Whatever you ask,' said Jeremiah.

'Tell the priest, when ye're passing the presbytery, to bring plenty of holy water with him if he's coming,' and he threw the Devil a knowing look. They were no more than gone when he stepped briskly to the wall.

The Devil spoke before he could say a word. 'What's that you said about holy water?'

There was a note of panic in his voice, though he tried to hide it.

'Ah, just that 'tis better to have all the tools o' the trade if you want a job done properly.'

A short silence.

'O' course, you needn't be here when he arrives,' Jack added, helpfully.

'But amn't I stuck here to this ... this ... How can I escape in time before he comes?'

Jack seemed amazed.

'Oh, if that's all that's wrong with you, why didn't you talk up sooner?'

'Why? Can you do something for me?'

'O' course I can. An' I'd be glad to. Anything to oblige an old friend.'

The Devil smiled, a doubtful little smile. His innocence did not extend as far as a belief in free gifts, but he still said: 'Do it, so ... I'd be thankful for it.'

Such an admission hurt, but there would be time later for a squaring of accounts.

'Well, now ...' Jack hesitated, 'there *is* a small thing – just a little detail, you know – that you might oblige us with.' When the Lad did not reply he continued. 'You remember, I'm sure, the seven years o' health, wealth an' happiness you gave us last time.'

The Devil's narrowed eyes showed that he did, all too clearly.

'Now, if you could see your way to giving us the same again, only for fourteen years this time, you could be down off o' that place like so,' and he snapped his fingers.

It was clear for the first time that hanging from his arms was beginning to cause him discomfort. He looked suddenly like someone who wanted in the worst way to scratch his nose, his ear or a place equally impossible. His jaw began to twitch, and his legs to tremble.

'Think about it if you want,' advised Jack, 'but don't take too long. The priest'll be here soon,' and then, as if apologising, 'But sorry. I was forgetting, you have a better view from up there than I have down here. You'll see him coming yourself.'

He turned towards the house.

'We'll see you soon. An' I hope you make the right decision. They tell me our man here, God bless an' keep him, is a terror entirely when he gets the holy water into his fist. Good luck to you when you meet him.'

'Stop where you are!'

The Devil's mind was fully made up if his voice was any sure guide.

'I'll do it. Only let me down out o' this.'

'You'll do what?' asked Jack mildly.

'I'll give you what you ask. Only release me now!'

'An' what is it we ask?'

Jack felt at that moment what a great barrister, or at least commissioner of oaths, had been lost in him.

'Fourteen years o' health, wealth an' happiness.'

'For who?'

'Yourself an' your ... wife, o' course,' panted the Devil. He was becoming exasperated, his eyes constantly on the road by the presbytery now.

'So you're giving me an' Máire fourteen years o' health, wealth an' happiness? Is that guaranteed?'

'It is. 'Tis! Now, let me off out o' here before I change my mind.'

His voice was rising dangerously. It would be stupid to push him any further, Jack knew.

'That's fine, so. Go back to where you came from, an' may luck go with you.'

He did not say which kind of luck he had in mind. Nor did the Old One wait to ask. He dropped like a sack of wet turf and lay dazed a moment. But only for a moment. He sprang up and fled without even a look back, his arms still stretched stiff above his head. He had seen what Jack could not: the black shape of the priest flapping towards them, a book in one hand, a bottle in the other and a crowd at his heels.

Jack was sitting on the wall when they arrived, sucking a blade of grass, the very picture of contentment. No one paid him much heed until there could be no doubt that the thing in the tree was there no longer. Only when this was certain did the priest address him, and in words not altogether friendly, either.

'Where is he?'

'Where's who, Father?' asked Jack innocently.

'You know well what I'm talking about. Don't mind pretending otherwise. I'd know it from your face.'

'I'd love to help you, Father – if I had any way o' doing it. But, sure, when you won't tell me ...'

The priest's eyes flashed. He was not a man who liked being made a fool of, especially in public. And there was a danger of that now, as he noted only too well in the eager faces all around.

'Go on out o' here, all o' ye,' he ordered suddenly, raising his hands as if to scatter geese. 'Myself an' this man have a bit o' business to transact. Private business. So be going, now – but thanks for all the help' – this last as a little sop to their disappointed looks as they shuffled off, muttering.

Jack was still chewing away, untroubled, when the priest turned again, his Sunday sermon face severely in place.

'Now,' he said evenly, 'I want to know, an' I'm putting you on your word as a Christian to tell me the truth, who was it above in the tree that they were telling me about? Was it who I think it was?'

'I'd say so,' Jack replied simply.

'In the name of ...' He caught himself. 'Don't you know from your catechism that you're supposed to have no dealings at all with that lad?'

The priest sounded baffled, as if the very notion of what Jack had done was beyond imagining.

'I do, Father, but he's gone now, an' not a bit o' harm done. Far from it, in fact.'

He levered himself off the wall.

'Come on up to the house. I have something to tell you an' show you, too.' However grumpily, the priest followed him in, and within ten minutes whatever book-objections had been bothering him were being soothed away by a third glass of brandy.

'Now, Father,' said Jack, all respect, when he saw the annoyance ebbing out of the other's countenance as the liquor ebbed in, 'you were telling us off the altar two Sundays ago about the gable wall o' the church, weren't you? 'Tisn't solid, you were saying. A fair bit o' work to be done on it.'

The priest nodded, unwilling to trust himself to words.

'Well, you'll have the devil's own work getting the money for that out o' the parish with times as bad as they are.'

The priest's face fell. He nodded again and his shoulders drooped.

'If you wouldn't mind taking a suggestion from a plain man like myself, I might be able to help you there.'

His reverence was interested now. He straightened in the chair. 'How so?'

'Tis like this.' Jack delicately searched for the correct words, eyeing Máire. 'We'd be prepared to make a ... donation ... of whatever money the job costs ...'

The priest's mouth seemed to have taken on a life of its own; it opened in a series of little clicks, wider and wider.

'... that is, if the thing below in the tree was ... ah ... forgotten about – after the place was blessed, o' course,' he added hurriedly.

Silence a moment. The priest's mouth closed, then smiled.

'The thing below in the tree? What thing? What tree? I don't even know what you're talking about.'

Jack smiled in return, and Máire. The bottle did its duty once again. And so the matter was settled.

'But first things first.' Jack rose. 'Maybe you'd need a few pounds in advance. To get the thing started, you know.'

The parish priest was so fuddled by this avalanche of good news that he could only shrug.

'Would you prefer it in sovereigns or notes?'

'Whatever is handiest to yourself,' the good man smiled. He was happy to be spared the sordid details of such transactions. Filthy lucre, after all, though sadly necessary, soiled the hands, left a sour tang where ideally the taste of sweetness should be.

Jack stepped into the bedroom and reappeared a moment later with a small wooden chest, held lovingly. He placed it on the table and nodded to Máire. She unclasped from her neck a gold chain on which a key hung, fitted the key to the chest, and there opened to the priest's eyes a sight to restore health to a sick man: a heap of bright coins, golden every last one. He reached out, touched them with trembling fingers, then caught himself. Avarice, greed, lust and the names of several other sins danced before his mind's eyes, but he quashed them manfully. 'The Lord's work comes first,' he muttered.

'What's that, Father?' Jack had half heard his words.

'Nothing. I was just saying to myself how the Lord works in strange ways.'

Jack was in full agreement. 'He does, indeed.'

Two fistfuls of sovereigns were soon jingling their way to the presbytery in the priest's pockets, with a promise of more to follow, and thus it was that the Devil's work repaired God's house, idle gossip was stilled, news of the strange apparition never spread beyond the parish bounds, and Jack and Máire continued to live as before, healthy, happy and charitable almost to a fault.

The years passed, as pass they tend to do, but there were three routines that Jack never allowed to vary: care for his old chair, the tending of the apple tree and the weekly examination of Máire's odds-and-ends bag in the wardrobe, which included renewing the mothballs whenever necessary.

Ten years galloped by. Eleven. Twelve. The thirteenth was no different. Nor the fourteenth. That summer they both took to the West Clare Railway and visited Kilkee for the first time, and marvelled at how the idle rich spent their leisure hours. It would provide them with stories enough for the filling of many a dark winter night, Jack confidently expected.

But before winter comes September. There is no evading that simple fact. Nor was Jack seeking to escape it, though he willingly enough put it from his mind whenever it became too insistent.

Their fateful day approached and they both waited wordlessly for what they knew must be: he *would* come. And he was sure to be very, very angry.

'I wouldn't blame him,' Jack nodded as they huddled at breakfast that morning. 'I think I'd feel the same way myself if I got the treatment that misfortune got.'

Máire almost laughed to hear this, but did not ask the question it begged.

'Men!' was all she said, and that to the silence in her own head.

At that moment – 'Thud! Thud! Thump!' – a sound they knew only too well filled the house. Their visitor was at the door, and this time he did not wait for it to be opened. With a crash and an unseemly yelp of glee he was in the room and leaped onto the table, scattering food and crockery. The teapot barely missed scalding Máire and she staggered back, almost tripping over her skirt. She was back in an instant, like a ti-gress, her voice fiery.

'Have you any manners at all, or what kind of a father an' mother reared you, you dirty bodach? If I had you here one week I'd teach you to know your place, you cníopaire.'

Once started, there was no stopping her, and even the Devil clapped his hands to his ears at last. Jack saw his chance, leaned across and touched a hairy arm. The Old One leaped.

'Surely 'tisn't nervous you are.' Jack was truly concerned.

'Tell her to shut up, will you? She'll drive us mad!'

'So, 'tis "us" now, eh?' thought Jack. 'There might be hope for me yet if I play this right.'

He turned to Máire and tapped a finger urgently several times to his lips.

'Shhh! That's enough said. We know what you mean, all right, now.'

She stopped in mid-tirade, amazed at the 'we'.

'Men,' she said again, this time aloud, and barged off, breathing heavily.

'You'll excuse her, I hope,' Jack pleaded. 'She isn't feeling herself these last couple o' days. We were expecting you sooner, you see. You kind o' surprised her, I think. But don't mind that now. I know why you're here, an' if you'll gimme one minute I'll just get my bag o' belongings – a few little things I might need, you know – an' I'll be with you.'

So surprised was the Devil by this odd contrast that though he looked Jack up and down suspiciously he made no objection to the request. And when Jack returned moments later, the bag tucked neatly under his oxter, there was no question, for Máire and the Devil were locked in a long stare. In fact it was Jack who had to pull him away.

'Come on,' he urged. 'I'm looking forward to meeting your family. An' I'm sure they're anxious to meet me too.'

A spell seemed to have been broken, for the Devil now locked on him directly, eye to eye, all his old fire back once more. He smiled, showing his yellow merciless teeth.

'I was inclined to forget, so I was. They're anxious to meet you, indeed – every one of 'em with a red-hot poker in his fist an' only waiting the command from me to stick it you-know-where.'

He clapped an iron grip on Jack, who now began to hope he had not said too much. Better to keep thinking positively, though, he told himself.

'We might as well be on our road, so,' and with one last 'Good luck. Pray for me' to Máire he set off under close escort, stepping out briskly, as if to Mass.

FOR OVER AN HOUR neither of them spoke. Then Jack asked permission for a short rest.

'No.'

As brief as that, and as final.

They walked on and still no let-up.

'My feet are all skinned. Stop, can't you, until I take off my socks?'

'No.'

Midday passed and Jack began to labour. The years of good feeding were now beginning to tell.

'I can't go any farther,' he wheezed. 'I'll have to stop or I'll get a heart-attack.'

The Devil chuckled at this notion.

'Why don't you?' he replied. 'It'd make my job a lot easier.'

Since it was obvious there was no respect here for age, or weight, a different approach was called for. Jack began to pray aloud. Slowly and deliberately, in the most pious voice he could summon. He had spoken only a few words when he was elbowed sharply in the ribs.

'Shut your mouth. I hate that kind o' dirty language.'

The Devil was genuinely angry. But Jack only raised his face, threw his eyes up to the heavens and prayed as if his whole future depended on it – which it did.

After several minutes of heavy breathing the Devil jammed his fingers in his ears, gave Jack a vicious kick in the shin and shouted: 'Any more of it, now, an' I'll throttle you where you stand. Not another step will you go, d'you hear?'

Jack stopped and glared at him.

'If you don't let me stop for a rest, 'tis worse I'll be getting. I can tell you that. You haven't a notion of all the prayers my mother taught me when I was a child. An' I remember every one of 'em.'

He burst into another blast of benediction and at that the Devil laid a trembling hand on his shoulder.

'All right,' he snarled. 'We'll take a minute's rest here. But only as long as you shut your mouth an' keep that dirty ráiméis to yourself.'

'Now, now!' Jack cautioned. 'That's no way to talk about holy words.' But he took the matter no further, and so they sat, Jack on a large stone, the Devil under a bush a few feet away, glowering and cursing under his breath.

'Ahhh!' Jack's sigh of relief was genuine enough. But though his feet were killing him and he was out of breath, his mind was whirling. And he knew precisely what he had to do next.

As if he were quite alone he began to unfold Máire's bag lovingly, shaking his head, smiling.

'What's that you're doing?' barked the Dark One.

Jack ignored that. Instead he enquired pleasantly: 'Tell me, did you ever play any games when you were a young lad?'

'What d'you mean "young lad"? What are you talking about, "games"?'

'Are you telling me you never played games, or that you were never young?'

'I know nothing about foolery like that,' hissed the Devil. 'You're annoying my ears, so shut up.'

'Hold on now a minute until I explain something to you, boyo. 'Tis little about civilised living you know, by the looks of it. But I'm the man that might educate you if you're able to listen. Now, when I was a young fellow we used to play a game called "Jump the Bag"...'

'I'm not interested,' interrupted the Devil. 'Stupid name, stupid game.'

'Well, I'm going to tell you about it, anyway. Sure, while we're here we might as well be doing something more than looking at each other – or d'you want me to start the prayers again?'

Since there was no response to this he shook out the bag, held it up at arms' length before him, open, and said, 'Ah, I'm not able to do it now, but when I was young an' supple – like you are now, God bless you –'

'Don't say that!' roared the Devil. 'I hate the mention of that fellow's name.'

'All right! All right!' Jack answered soothingly. 'You're very touchy, aren't you? But don't mind that. Look! As I was saying, when I was young we used to play this game, an' all you had to do was jump into the bag, jump out o' the bag, an' keep that up for as long as you were able – all the time holding the bag at the length o' your arms in front o' you. Not as easy as it might seem.'

'A stupid game for stupid fools,' was the Devil's only reply, but Jack could see that there was a flicker of interest there.

'Is that so?' he sneered. 'Easy to say that, but could you do it yourself?' He guessed that the Devil's vanity might get the better of him, and he was correct: the Old One did not take kindly to being told what he could or could not do.

'What is it you're babbling about, boy? Gimme that rag of a bag, an' I'll show you something.'

He snatched the bag, held it out at arms' length, then leaped nimbly into it. It came up to his chest.

'What about that? Hah!' he laughed scornfully. Jack laughed too.

'Ah, that's the easy bit. But jump out now as fast.'

He did so.

'Very good. Only how many times can you do it in a minute? That'll be the test. I could do it forty-three times a minute when I was about your age.'

The Devil began a frenzied leaping in and out, urged on – 'Faster! Faster!' – by Jack. If any passers-by had seen him there they would have said he was surely an escapee from the madhouse.

But Jack, though he was enjoying the sight of the Devil making an idiot of himself, was watching carefully his every move, awaiting his opportunity. It came when he noticed the Devil's tongue appearing at the corner of his mouth. He was beginning to tire, no doubt of that. Carefully selecting his moment, when the Old One was disappearing into the bag, Jack put out his foot, tripped him, and he fell heavily, still trying to hold up the top of the sack.

'Oh, Lord,' cried Jack, all helpfulness, 'are you hurt? Here, let go an' I'll hold this for you while you're getting up.'

So saying, he snatched the two top corners of the bag,

twisted them into a solid knot, doubled it and tied it tighter again with a length of twine which, by the grace of God, just happened to be in his pocket.

'There you are inside now,' he whooped, 'an' 'tis there you'll stay until you promise to go away back to Hell an' bother the two of us no more.'

The Devil was having none of this. With a shriek of fury, he attacked the bag, tried to burn, eat and kick his way out of it. But all in vain. Even his power was useless against that wondrous material.

All Jack did was to heave the bag over his shoulder and take to the road, with the Devil kicking inside it like a calf. But Jack never felt a thing; he had a fine layer of fat to protect him after twenty-eight years of leisure and good feeding.

Whistling as he went, he kept walking until he came to a mill. There was no sign of activity, but he went to the door and knocked. The miller came out.

'God bless you, sir,' smiled Jack, using his most ingratiating tone of voice. 'I have a small little bag of oats here, an' I'd appreciate it if you'd grind it for me.'

The miller looked him up and down doubtfully.

'Please, sir. I have a young family at home an' my poor wife can hardly keep 'em fed. I'd be thankful to you forever if you'd oblige me –'

'Look, I don't do small quantities like that – not worth my while.'

'Oh, please do, sir. Just this one time. Please! I'm begging you, an' 'tisn't often I beg.'

Jack felt himself warming to his task, and raised his voice.

'For the sake o' the poor little orphans, sir.'

The miller put his fingers in his ears, obviously disgusted.

'All right! Just shut your mouth an' I'll see what I can do.'

Sulkily, he beckoned Jack in.

'But you'll have to do the job yourself. I was just goin' for my dinner, an' I'm still goin'.'

'I'd be delighted,' said Jack. 'I'd hate to keep any man from the table. Only show me where the millstones are, an' I'll see to it.'

That was done, and in the room where the great round stones were about their endless circling Jack looked around him, full of admiration.

'This is a fine place an' no doubt about it,' he nodded to the miller approvingly. 'But, look, I know what to do. Go on an' eat your dinner for yourself. An' thanks.'

The miller plodded off, and Jack went at once about his business. He swung the sack onto the floor and without ceremony asked one brief question: 'Will you go away an' leave us alone, an' not come back no more?'

His answer was a well-known phrase, one of its two words containing four letters, Jack sighed, but said no more, only pushed the bag onto the flat stone and waited for the inevitable, a look of pain on his face. In a few seconds the two great stones were drawing the bag inexorably in, inch by inch. For a moment there was a startled silence, then a yell, followed by a shriek as first one leg, then the other, was crushed. The huge stones never faltered, only ate up the bag, until they came to the Devil's head. That was a nut too hard to crack. In fact it was the vertical stone that cracked, from top to bottom. But Jack had little time either to gloat or wonder; the miller was back now, spluttering his dinner to every side of him in rage. His roars could be heard in the next parish as he shook the floor in his fury.

'God's curse on you! My new millstone is destroyed, the one that came from France only last month. I'll kill you for this! Stand there until I get the hatchet, you low sleeveen.'

He thundered off, intent on bodily harm, but Jack had no intention of waiting to be chopped into small pieces. He snatched up the bag, legged it out the door, and no fear that the miller caught up with him, either; amazing what a turn of speed even the old or overweight can discover in the face of the threat of a blunt instrument, or one with an edge.

After half a mile of road he had to stop, exhausted. He held out the sack and shook it.

'Hi! Are you still in one piece in there, poor man?'

A weak groan was all the answer he got.

'Good. You're alive, anyway. Now, 'tis time to talk serious business again. I'll ask you what I asked you before: if I let you out, will you promise to go away once an' for all, an' not bother us again, ever?'

'I won't,' croaked the Devil. 'But what I *will* do is kill you slowly – roast you – when I get you home. You'll be three hundred years dying.'

Jack sighed.

'You're a hard one to teach sense to, an' no two ways about it. But it can be done. An' it *will*. Be sure o' that.'

He swung the bag onto his back again and walked until he came to a quarry. He could hear the noise of the stone-crushing machine a half-mile away and he smiled, but when he came in sight of the busy scene he almost laughed aloud. For his mind was working on a new trial for the prisoner in his sack.

At the quarry-face he saw up to fifty men sweating, hacking at the rock with sledgehammers and pickaxes, while others carted away the fallen stone in barrows and dumped it onto a clattering, swaying conveyor-belt which carried it to the terrible crusher where it was reduced to manageable size for road-fill or building or whatever.

Without delay Jack's keen eye picked out the man he was looking for, the only one standing up without an implement in his hands – the foreman, surely. He inched his way carefully towards him, making a great deal of the sack on his back, as if it were sorely pressing him down.

'Sir!' He tapped the foreman's shoulder.

'Well?' said he, impatient. 'Who are you? What d'you want?'

'Just a small thing only, sir.'

He laid down the bag.

'I'm putting a few stones in front o' the house at home, but they're too big an' people'll be tripping over 'em. Any chance I could grind 'em up here? It'd save me the bother o' having to break 'em with a hammer. I have a bad back, you see.'

The foreman examined him up and down, then noted the bag. Was this another of those scattered fellows who were more and more infesting the roads since that cursed Poor Law was changed, he wondered. But all his doubts were silenced when Jack passed him a half-crown – a goodly sum in those days – with, 'but I wouldn't want to be putting your valuable time astray, so here's a little something for yourself.'

The foreman's whole attitude changed. He winked and tipped his finger to his cap.

'You're more than welcome. Throw it up there on the belt. 'Tis no trouble at all.'

Jack did so, and followed at his leisure as the bag bumped along. Naturally enough, when the Devil, in the darkness of the sack, heard the clattering growing louder his ears pricked up. He could make neither head nor tail of it, though his alarm increased as the noise grew louder.

'Are you sure you won't change what's left o' your mind?' asked Jack one last time, three feet from the machine.

No reply.

With a sigh he watched the bag topple into the iron mouth of the crusher and even he flinched as he watched the huge jagged teeth do their work.

There was only a single squawk out of the Devil, and that sliced off suddenly. Then silence.

Jack waited by the second belt at the back of the machine, but what he saw, far from giving him pleasure, almost made him sympathise with the Devil. Anyone so stupid, so proud, was under a severe disability, indeed. For though the bag was still mostly intact, through several holes he could make out various bits and pieces of crushed and broken limbs, skin and hair at impossible angles and dark blood beginning to soak through the fabric.

He picked up the tattered thing cautiously, excitement beginning to get the better of his disgust.

'Are you ready to talk to me now? Or will I put you through it again?'

Only a long, pitiful groan from the bag.

'That isn't an answer. Are you saying "yes" or "no" to me?'

'The only reply you'll get from me is the one you got already. I was alive before you were ever thought of, an' I'll still be there, even if I'm crippled, when you're fried into a bit o' blackened meat on the hobs o' Hell.'

Jack would have put the bag through the crusher again, and again if necessary, but just then a long succession of rocks began to arrive down the belt. The foreman arrived also.

'All right, now. Move back there. No more time for small jobs. The job we're at must go on,' and he shoved Jack away.

He had no choice but to take to the road again, tiresome though it might be.

'Maybe I'm as well off,' he consoled himself. 'If that machine didn't work on him the first time there's little chance of it doing the job a second or third time around.'

So he toiled on, for what seemed like several miles, until he came to a forge. No ordinary forge, either, for in the yard were four huge apprentice smiths, fine muscular fellows, flattening a massive sheet of iron on the ground – making a yard-gate for some landlord or other, it could be – one of them after the other landing his crashing mighty blow in a heavy solid rhythm.

Jack watched this display of co-operation and strength for several minutes, mesmerised. Then one of them noticed him and stopped. The rhythm was broken and with it the spell that had kept them apart, in their separate worlds.

'God bless the work, men,' Jack got in hurriedly. 'I was watching ye there an' I couldn't but admire the strength o' ye.'

They were all staring at him by now, sweat gathering in pools around them, glad enough of the rest, maybe, though none of them said so.

Jack, seeing that he had their attention, hurried on.

'An' maybe strong men like ye might be able to do a tiny little bit of a job for me.'

'What is it?' the broadest of them asked.

'I have a small piece o' scrap metal here in my bag an' 'tis sticking into me an' cutting the back off o' me. Any chance ye'd flatten it out for me an' make my walking o' the roads a bit more comfortable?'

'Anything to oblige a traveller,' they murmured, sympathetic. 'Throw it down there, an' we'll see what we can do.'

This time the Devil was asked no question, only dumped onto the sheet of iron, and at once the smiths began to rain blows down on the bag, every one heavier and more accurate than the one before. But only five or six had connected when they noticed that the bag was moving, that something seemed to be squirming inside it. Jack saw them hesitate and moved quickly.

'Begod, lads, ye'll have to do a bit better than this. All ye're doing is moving it around.'

'Tisn't us that's doing that at all. But *something* is moving it!'

'Yerra, that's only the oul' iron vibrating. What else could it be? Hit it again an' ye'll see.'

One of them put his boot to the bag and tapped it.

'There's no sound o' metal out o' this.'

'How could there be? 'Tis nearly all lead that's in it,' Jack countered, his mind racing. 'But if big men the like o' ye aren't able to flatten a bit o' lead 'tis a poor kind of a story. I'll call into the next school I meet an' maybe the young scholars might do it for me instead.'

He made to pick up the bag, but the man nearest him kicked his hand away.

'Keep back out o' that,' he snarled, 'an' let me get a right welt at it. I'll flatten it out myself.'

'After I'm finished, maybe,' interrupted his companion.

'You won't finish anything until I have first crack at it,' snorted the third.

'Ye're full o' talk, but that's all,' said the fourth, raising his hammer. 'I'm the only one here fit to do this. An' I will!'

There was a dull thud as the four hammers met, paused in mid-air, then with a mighty whoosh all came down together. This time there was no mistake. They landed, each of them, squarely on the Devil, but if they did he shrieked – 'Aiiyee!' – and leaped four feet into the air. The smiths leaped, too, ten feet backwards, shocked.

'Damn it,' gasped one of them, 'that thing must be bewitched. The Devil himself must be in it.'

'Yerra, indeed he isn't, or in it,' Jack mocked. 'Will ye go on an' hit it again – or is it so ye're afraid?'

Before they could reply the master smith, the owner of the forge, stuck his head round the jamb of the forge door, and froze when he saw his men standing idle, gaping at a bag. He strode forward.

'What in God's name is going on here?' he barked. 'Why aren't ye at work?'

'Ask him.'

They all pointed at Jack.

'Who are you, stranger?' he thundered. 'An' what're you doing here, distracting my men?' and when Jack had no immediate reply to this, he added: 'Short o' words, are you? Well, I hope you're not short o' money.' 'Cos you're the one that's going to pay for this. You know the oul' saying "time is money", so cough up.'

Jack laughed to his face.

'You can scratch your backside. These men here were only doing me a good turn. I'll pay you nothing.'

'What's that you're after saying?' The smith was obviously not used to being answered so. 'Repeat it – if you want to die a sudden death.'

'I will. I said you could scratch your backside. But you can scratch any other part o' yourself if it suits you better.'

The smith stood, looking about him wildly, clenching and unclenching his fingers, like a man fit to be tied. Then he turned, dashed into the forge and reappeared in seconds with a red-hot poker clutched trembling before him.

'Now we'll see whether you'll pay or not,' he hissed, lunging at Jack, who raised the bag – the first thing he could think of – to protect himself. The Devil's luck was out that day, and his left eye also now, for the poker and bag collided at one of the holes from which he was now peeping out, terrified.

All previous screams were as whispers of joy compared to the bellow of agony and horror that now echoed through that yard. It froze the very marrow of the five swarthy men; even Jack, though he was nearly accustomed to this kind of thing now, felt a tremor. But that did not prevent him from getting himself away fast – as fast as he had ever moved – excusing himself weakly over his shoulder as he went, and snatching up a fine two-pound hammer lying there, to defend himself with if necessary.

From the gateway he struggled, without looking behind to see if he was followed. But there was no fear of that. It would be at least an hour before any of the smiths were in a way to stir, never mind try to pursue him. In fact, none of them was the better of their experience for well over a year after, and the smith's wife even had to take up the trade while her husband confined himself to making the tea, so shaky had his hands become.

Jack never stopped until the forge was well and truly out of sight, and then only after he had looked cautiously all about. He sat on the road-wall and laid the bag gently at his feet.

'Well, my man, are you still refusing to make a new bargain with me? Or will I have to take you to meet more o' my friends?'

The answer was instant, pleading and heart-rending.

'Please, let me out o' this cursed bag. Please! My eye is out, I can only see with one half o' me, an' every bone that's in me is broke.'

Jack shook his head vehemently.

'No! An' d'you know something else? The next place I'm taking you is three times worse than any o' the ones you were in already. So talk fast, 'cos once I start walking I won't stop.'

'You have it! Anything you'll ask. Only let me out.'

'That's the kind o' talk I like to hear,' smiled Jack, 'but tell it to me again – slowly.'

'I'll go away, an' I'll never bother yourself or your wife again. Now, open this ******* thing!'

Jack crossed himself, but there was nothing to be gained by holding out for too much. He slowly undid the knotted top of the bag and shook out the contents. What fell to the road was not a pleasant or presentable sight. It looked, for all the world, like an animal that had been gone over by a week's traffic on a busy highway, tattered, flattened and broken. To tell hands from heels was no easy task.

Jack stared at it, pop-eyed. But for a moment only. No sooner did the bloody mass touch the ground than a cloud of steam and smoke combined gushed up with a mighty hiss, and when it cleared enough to allow a view, Jack found only a hole before him. He approached the edge cautiously, and peered down into it. But there was no seeing to the depths of it.

'By the Lord, but wasn't he in a big hurry home,?' was the only comment he could think of. And there was little more to be said, for that was exactly what had happened: the Old One, what remained of him, had lost all interest in the doings of this world and taken the shortest route to the Place Beneath.

There was nothing further to hold Jack there. He folded the bag and with a little skip set off for home. Máire was waiting anxiously at the gate. When she saw who was there she ran to meet him and, for the first and last time ever in public, threw her arms around him and hugged him.

'I don't know how you did it, or even what you did, but welcome home anyway.'

The temptation to build a tale of noble and valiant deeds fluttered for an instant before Jack, but he knew that Máire would not be easily fooled, so he contented himself for the moment with a more or less accurate account of what had happened. She was no less impressed and pleased by that, for she listened intently to every word and at the end of the tale she climbed to her feet and cried, 'We'll have to have a celebration, an' what better than a céilí?'

And so it was: invitations were scattered throughout the parish, food and drink delivered, and musicians hired.

That night, one of the greatest crowds ever seen in Cratloe assembled at the McCarthy house. An open house it was, too, with no shortage of anything that could help make the céilí stick in the memory. Jack was the centre of attention, everyone wanting to talk with him, drink his health or dance with him – even the men.

But it was this last that brought about the tragedy for which that same céilí was ever afterwards remembered. For after dancing six sets in a row he staggered, clapped his hands to his chest, let out a gurgle and fell, dead, of a heart-attack.

And so the night's entertainment was ruined. And so also Jack went to his hereafter. But no ordinary hereafter, for when he found his otherworldly feet and when the dust had settled he noted that there were two stairways near him, one up and one down. Not for a minute did he hesitate, only dusted himself off and began to climb upward. And no easy climb it was, either. But at last he saw a door above, though hardly welcoming, for it was studded with black iron knobs and there was no handle or latch of any sort.

For a few moments he stood panting, then, when there was no sign of life, rapped on it with his fist.

No reply.

He tried again, harder this time, but succeeded only in bloodying his knuckles.

'Blast this, anyway,' he growled, annoyed. 'Is there anyone at all in the cursed place?'

He was just about to plant a kick on the timber-work when a slight movement stopped him, then another. In a moment the door had been jerked inward and there, staring at him, stood a thick-set, bearded man dressed in a sweet-smelling robe. Jack, though startled, jumped to an immediate conclusion: 'Would you be St Peter by any chance?'

'I would. An' you'd be Jack Murt from Cratloe, by the look o' you.'

'The very man. But here, we can talk about all that another time. Why don't you be a bit neighbourly an' leave me in
out o' the cold while we're getting to know each other?

'There'll be no in here for you, wherever else you'll go,'
rasped Peter, holding up his crozier threateningly.

Jack's mouth fell open.

'Why not?' he cried. 'Amn't I as entitled as the next Christian to see Heaven?'

Peter let out a scairt of laughter, but there was no mirth
in it.

'You! Is it you? A villain that did nothing except consort
with the Old Lad while you were in the world, an' you expect
to be let in up here? Go on out o' this at once, before I lose
my temper an' do something with this crozier that 'twas never
intended for. Go down that other stairs as far as it'll take you.
Your room is booked an' waiting for you in the Dark Haunt,
an' the heating is turned up full – or so I'm told.'

And so saying he turned on his heel, slammed the door
and Jack was left by himself to consider what best to do.

He shrugged, sighed, then did the only thing left: trudged
down, down, down the stairway of shadows to the nether
place. It was not pleasant. Hotter and hotter it grew until he
could hardly breathe. But still more steps stretched down,
though increasingly flecked with crimson. His feet began to
sweat, then to hurt. He tried to walk on the edges of his shoes,
concentrating only on the next step until at last he was teeter-
ing in a sort of corridor. Before him was a door and outside
that door were scattered bones, rags and hair. And when his
fuddled gaze fixed itself on the metalwork itself – no timber
would survive long here – it stuck there, for on it were spread
no less than four bodies, crucified. And worse, they were still
alive, slobbering, weeping and leaking onto the red-hot flag-
stones, sending spurts of steam towards the ugly ceiling. Jack

groaned, shivered, then shook himself. His Clareness began to resurface.

'What the hell am I thinking of?' he gritted. 'Isn't the Fair of Spancilhill thirteen times worse than anything that's here? Any man that faced that could face this, too, surely.'

He threw up his eyes, hopped the last few steps to the door and tapped, grimacing at the wretches hanging there, trying not to meet their pleading eyes.

No answer.

He knocked again, louder. Still no answer.

'Only one way to get this crowd's attention,' he snarled, snatching from his belt the two-pound hammer that he had picked up at the forge. He landed one blow, then another and another on the dark metal, and kept up the racket until a little window overhead – more a porthole than a window – snapped open. A head was thrust out and an angry, but young voice shouted down.

'Who are you, what're you doin' here, and why're you kick-in' our door?'

It was one of the Devil's younger sons, on sentry-duty, no doubt.

'I have an appointment with your father, boyeen. Go in an' tell him Jack Murt from Cratloe is here. An' be quick about it!'

The little devil puckered up his brow, unsure what to do in face of such effrontery – or was it confidence? He scowled, just as he had seen his parent do so often at this very place, but Jack raised the hammer and shook it.

'Go on, quick, or you'll get this between the eyes.'

He regretted having to threaten a child, and he knew too that he was pushing his luck, but what was to be lost at this late stage?

The window was clapped shut, footsteps pattered down

inside and a few moments later Jack heard voices in a muttered conversation. He leaned as close to the door as the heat allowed and could make out snatches of what sounded like an argument:

'... Don't tell me he's here, that cursed liúdramán. He's the one that put out my eye. Tell him I'm not at home at all.'

'But he knows ...'

'I don't care. We're not letting him into this house an' that's that. He'll destroy us if he gets his ugly head inside the door, an' I won't ...'

After a very few minutes the young devil's head popped out above again. He was close to crying.

'He don't want to see you,' he whined, 'an' anyway, he says he isn't at home.'

The window was slammed before Jack could add a word to this. He was left once more in the gloom of that sweaty corridor.

'They don't want me. That's all about it,' he sighed, turning away, a flicker of a smile dimpling his cheeks. 'Nothing for it, I s'pose, except to try the place above again an' hope there's a bit more Christianity there this time.'

Cautiously he made his way back up towards the light, every step drawing a deeper sigh from his old lungs, his pauses growing ever more frequent.

When the Pearly Gateway once again faced him he was almost past caring, but he summoned up his final ounces of energy to totter towards it.

He leaned on the Sacred Stones with both hands, head bowed, panting, then turned, slithered to the ground and sat there motionless, wordless. For a moment only, though. A voice boomed out close by, a voice he had heard very recently.

'Don't tell me you're here again. Didn't I order you to go down to the place below?'

There was precious little of welcome in the rasping tones.

Looking up, Jack saw St Peter, hands on hips, glowering at him. He blinked, mouth open, then rolled painfully onto his knees, ready to pray if that was what was required.

'You wouldn't want me spending the rest o' my time in a dark hole the like o' that, surely,' he answered weakly.

'It has nothing to do with me,' said Peter. 'I'm only in charge o' this gate. Remember that when they're heating you below.'

'But I thought there was supposed to be things like Mercy an' Love an' Forgiveness up here.' Jack hoped he sounded indignant, but could no longer be sure, so exhausted was he.

Peter threw him a dirty glare.

'I won't bother going through the ins and outs of it with you now, 'cos not one bit o' difference is it going to make. All I'm telling you is that you'll have to go, an' go this minute.'

'But you can't ... I mean ... I'm an Irishman, amn't I? Is St Patrick inside? Or St Brigid, or Mochulla of Tulla. Any o' them holy people won't see me sent to a place as ugly as that.'

Peter looked suddenly old, as well as thoroughly sick of this conversation.

'For the last time, you're going down out o' here. That's all about it. They can't help you, so don't embarrass 'em by mentioning it.'

'I'll believe that when I hear it from their own mouths, not before, so bring 'em out. If you do that much I'll ask no more o' you.'

Peter hesitated just an instant, but it was enough to give Jack a final straw to grasp at.

'When they find out that one o' their own countrymen was treated like a piece o' dirt – an' in the wrong, too – there'll be another war in there' – he jabbed his finger towards the Gateway – 'even worse than one ye had before. The Irish are one big family, no matter what world they're in. You know little if you don't know that much. But if you don't you'll find it out shortly.'

Peter looked worried now, darted his eyes here and there, then stared long and hard at Jack.

'Hm ... Wait there until I find out what the rule-book says.'

He retreated several paces inside the Gateway, reached into a small cubby-hole and tugged out a huge leather-bound tome. Its weight staggered him and Jack was about to jump to his assistance when a vicious scowl stopped him in his tracks.

'Stay where you are,' Peter ordered. 'You can't pass that threshold until I consult the Book o' the Blest here.'

Jack wilted. He was beginning to have doubts about this Heaven place. If it made no allowance for a person's good and helpful impulses what would it be like to spend the rest of eternity in? Not very satisfying, it seemed. But better to smile and say nothing just yet, he decided.

Peter, gasping, stumbled to a desk on the left-hand side of the short corridor, let down the book in a whumph of dust, then opened the brass clasps weakly. Any enthusiasm he might ever have had for this type of work was long gone. Jack could see that much clearly. Yet ... yet ... his whole future was depending on the next few moments. He could not stand by and not intervene in some positive way. He shook himself, and stepped forward.

'Here, let me give you a hand with that ...'

'Not an inch farther!' ordered Peter. 'I have enough on my hands with this. Another move an' you'll stay out there for good, even if you have a right to be in. I'm in no humour now for arguing. So don't put me to it.'

Jack shrugged, sighed and decided to wait.

'What's that your name is again?'

Peter aimed yet another poisonous glare at Jack.

'Jack McCarthy from Cratloe, County Clare. My father was a ...'

'I'm not interested in your father one way or another!' snarled Peter. ''Tis yourself that's in the balance here now, so wait until you're spoken to.'

Pages were riffled then, with a weary lack of interest, Peter's fingernail scraping along list after list: 'K ... L ... M ... N ...'

'Hold on, there! Stop! You're gone past the mark. Is it so you can't read, or what?' shouted Jack, indignant.

'Oh, I can read all right,' Peter replied absently, and then looked at Jack in an odd manner.

'Then what's wrong with you? Read out my name, an' no more about it.'

Peter glanced at the book again, then smiled, a slow, broadening grin.

'I can't read out what isn't there,' he declared flatly.

'What d'you mean, not there?'

'Just that. Not here. So I'm afraid I'll have to say bye-bye to you – now!'

There was a cold knife-edge to his voice.

He turned, clapped his hands, and immediately there appeared at his side two well-dressed, gentlemanly-looking types.

'Angels, no doubt,' groaned Jack, 'or maybe some o' them archangel fellows we learned about in sixth class. But what the hell does it matter? I'm sunk, unless ...'

His thoughts settled, frighteningly clear all of a sudden, on the one appeal he could still hope to make when all others had failed: St Peter might still not have forgotten that he had once been human.

'D'you remember that leaky oul' boat you had in the Sea o' Galilee with the red cloak you stole off of a drunk Roman for a sail? An' that huge fish you poached the time your father was sick in bed – the one you sold to buy the medicine with?'

Where it came from he had not the foggiest notion – it amazed him utterly – but this information had an electric effect on St Peter. He stiffened. His head jerked up. Mouth open, obviously confused, he stared.

When his voice came to him, it was a squawk.

'How do *you* know ..?'

'There are things,' Jack intoned, trying to hide his own bewilderment, 'that are hidden from the blest that only the truly Blessed can see. Or people from Ireland. An' while I'm not claiming anything great for myself ...'

'All right! All right!' Peter flapped his hands weakly. 'You have your point made. I'll consult The Man Inside an' see what His verdict is. Wait here!'

He turned before disappearing round the corner.

'An' this is the final word, mind.'

Jack relaxed, since nothing else was to be done, and began to whistle a little tune, as much to cheer himself as to convince anyone who might be listening that here was a confident soul.

And someone was, for within a few seconds a little window over the Gate – the exact equivalent of the one in the Place Below – was opened and an old man's head and shoulders appeared. His finger was to his lips.

'Shhh!' he whispered. 'Listen. Don't say a word. I'm Saint Mochulla of Tulla. If you're wondering where them words you spoke to Peter came from, wonder no more.'

He cackled, but suppressed it quickly.

'Now listen to me. If you have any sense, stay out o' here. 'Tis the most ... most ...'

He seemed to be having trouble getting the word out, whatever it was, darting his eyes about, looking frightened of a sudden.

''Tis what?' urged Jack. 'I'm not following you.'

'Tis the most monotonous cursed place anyone could be in,' sobbed Mochulla, collapsing limply over the window-sill. 'An' I'm stuck here for the rest of eternity, singing oul' hymns that don't even rhyme, bowing an' scraping to a crowd o' thool-ramawns that call themselves my betters, an' who think they *are* better than me, what's more, 'cos I'm only from a "rabbit-hole the like o' Tulla", as they call it. If I only knew what I was letting myself in for up here I'd have committed a couple o' robberies at least in Tulla, an' maybe even worse. But I'm caught here now. No going back for me. But you're not in yet. An' if you have any sense you won't be. Whatever else you do, stay out of it if you have any respect for yourself. An' good luck to you.'

He slammed out the little window without one word more, leaving Jack with much to think of and far too little time to do so.

'It'd be a foolish thing not to trust a Clareman, I'm thinking. An' a saint, moreover,' he muttered. 'I wouldn't have a minute's luck for it,' and a saying of his dead mother came to mind: 'What's near to home is near the bone.' That decided him.

Accordingly, when Peter appeared in the little corridor, smiling, a few moments later and broke the good news, a surprise awaited him.

'Praise an' bless His Divine Highness for ever more, McCarthy! You're in. He's to allow an exception in your case.'

'Safer for him,' thought Jack. 'Or they'd never again see a wink o' sleep in there.'

But he held his peace. All he replied was, 'Hmmm. This'll have to be considered. I'll take a few turns around the yard here an' I'll tell you when I have my mind made up. I won't be too long,' and off he went, hands behind back and brow furrowed.

Peter gawped. Democracy was a concept he had no experience of. Foolishness, though, he recognised at first sight.

'Get your ugly miserable skin in here – NOW! – or I'll

take it on myself to carry out His blessed orders in a way you won't like.'

Jack was all mildness when he answered.

'Thanks very much, sir. I appreciate your good wish for me. But I'll stay out, if you don't mind. I'll go down to the Place Below again. If I keep working on the door with my hammer long enough they'll let me in, I'd say. There's a pile o' people in there that I'd prefer to be talking to than the crowd in here.' Jack made this decision, even after a brief recollection of some of the hardy old backbiters and hypocrites who used to inhabit the chapel in Cratloe, swathed in prayers and beads in it, all bloodthirsty outside.

'Gimme a straightforward blackguard over an angel any day o' the week. At least I'd know how to handle him,' he thought, then held out his hand, all regret.

'So goodbye. 'Twas nice meeting you, after all I heard about you.'

'But ... but ... you can't!' spluttered Peter as Jack turned to go. 'What'll Our Master think o' this? 'Tis a thing unheard of. I'll be thrown out myself.'

'What I'm doing is no reflection on you at all, Peter. 'Tis my decision, an' mine alone.'

'But ... please! Not down *there*, of all places. If you have any respect for *me*.'

He sounded near to tears.

'But where else have I to go?'

'No place ... except ... except ...'

A faraway look crept into Peter's eyes, followed by a mischievous little smile, well hidden from Jack behind his beard.

'Stand there a minute. I think there might be a finish to this that'll keep us all happy.'

'I hope there is,' sighed Jack, 'but show it to me quick, 'cos my mind is made up.'

Again Peter disappeared round the corner. He was back within a minute, a little man in tow who looked more like a large ball with legs than any person Jack had ever seen.

'How would you like this fellow as company in your travels?'

Jack said nothing, only eyed the creature suspiciously.

'Well?' Peter was impatient.

'I don't see how ...'

'Ah, you don't see, eh? Is that your bother? Well, maybe this'll help you –' and Peter reached into a small alcove and brought out a little brass lamp.

'You might need this since you're going down out o' here,' and he passed it to the fat dwarf. 'In fact, you'll need the both of 'em.'

'Why would I? Is it so you think my eyes aren't comrades, or what?'

'Take it, anyway. It could be a big help to you ... as well as to others.'

'I won't.'

'Look!' snarled Peter. 'The only reason I'm offering it to you is because I kind o' like you. An' after what your people did to my people in Limerick that's no small thing. So don't abuse my hospitality, if you value yourself.'

The way he said this – without the slightest trace of mirth – made Jack squint at him more closely. He saw nothing to reassure him, only a hand holding a lamp.

'I'm finished with you from this out. Go wherever you want. But if you have no light to guide you, there's many a dark thing in wait for you. An' even with this lamp there's no guarantee that you'll find what you're looking for – if you even know what that is.'

He turned to the dwarf.

'Light that, Fungusball, an' guide him to the place appointed. Nowhere else.'

'Place appointed?' cried Jack. 'But you said I was free to ...'

'Shut up! You have no further say in this.'

He ordered the dwarf again to light the lamp, and the little man obliged by opening his mouth wide, revealing a set of vicious-looking pike's fangs. One sideways twitch of his jaw sent out a flurry of sparks, one of which landed in the lamp, lighting there a little spurt of blue flame. It was obviously a well-practised operation for he seemed not at all surprised at his accuracy. Instead he wheeled, snorted and clamped a leathery crúb on Jack's left arm, then with a strength which there was no resisting, began to drag him away.

Peter took no further part in the proceedings except to squeeze the lamp into Jack's other hand, then turned wearily and walked off. The Pearly Gate clicked shut behind him and that was the last Jack ever saw of him.

And now it began to dawn on the same Jack that he had brought on himself something that he could no longer control, or even hope to. For the hand that was clamped on him was as cold and unyielding as steel. Along the corridor, then down the dark stairway he was dragged, digging in now his heels, now his toes as he squirmed this way and that, resisting every step of the way. But his protests were useless. The dwarf, whose width was almost that of the stairwell, ignored pleas, questions and finally even his curses; he seemed preoccupied with something else entirely.

'Why the hell do I need this gombo to bring me down here?' Jack whimpered to himself, furious. 'Wasn't I coming fine o' my own accord?'

But ... he was mistaken if he thought he was being escorted to the Lower Region, for less than halfway down his captor stopped without warning, clutched him even more tightly, then gripped the wall on the left-hand side, snickering. At once a door of sorts rattled aside, revealing a blackness. He glanced over his shoulder and tugged Jack closer to him.

'We – Here. This – You – Place. Go – Now. In. Good – Bye, Bad – Boy.'

He clumped down two steps more, forcefully, quickly, then yanked Jack over his head and into darkness that was too dark by far, a space that was world-wide yet coffin-narrow all at once.

He fell ... fell ... attempted to shriek. But nothing came, only a gurgling croak. How long, how far he fell he never after could recall; he knew nothing of it, for his senses left him after the first few seconds. So when he woke and raised his head timidly, imagine his confusion to find himself lying on the road outside Sixmilebridge graveyard.

He might, there and then, have concluded that the whole affair was no more than a bad nightmare, except for one thing: the little lamp glowing blue in his hand. Absently, still too preoccupied with getting his bearings, he attempted to snuff it out. But it would not be quenched, no matter how he tried with either breath, spit or his fingers. He was about to fling it from him when a movement on the road some distance away distracted him. He froze and stared. Two men were coming in his direction, both on bicycles, and each the worse for drink, it seemed, for they were wobbling this way and that, talking in loud, silly snorts and guffaws. Jack recognised them immediately: Seán O'Keeffe and Brian Gleeson, two old drinking-cronies of his. He leaped up, delighted, waving his arms to stop them.

And stop they did. Suddenly. Then with hardly a glance at each other they sprang from their bicycles, flung them aside and fled, roaring. Never had two men sobered up so quickly.

'Wait!' Jack yelled. 'Come back! Why so are ye running?'

But they were gone and only the echoes of his own question answered him. Puzzled, he began to walk, more quickly with every step, towards home. Rest and a hot meal; yes, and a talk with his wife. That would do much to put these events in some kind of order, he told himself.

Yet ... yet ... everything was not as it should be. Two more times he met travellers on the road and both times he saluted and gave them a friendly greeting. But the reaction was the same, and instant, in each case: a long, open-mouthed stare, quick sign of the cross, and then helter-skelter retreat.

'Is the whole world gone mad, or what?' he breathed, scratching his neck in wonder. It had not yet dawned on him that the cause might be himself, not the rest of the world.

But if there was not the flicker of a doubt in his mind before, the reaction he got when he arrived at his own front door left him in no doubt that something was seriously amiss. His wife it was that opened it, certainly, but her response was not that of the Máire he knew – calm, welcoming and good-humoured. Instead, her hand jerked away as if she had been burned and she began to back into the kitchen.

'No! Get off away o' here, whatever you are!' And she bless-ed herself. Jack's temper was rising now. He had had more than enough of this foolery. He was tired. All he wanted to do was have a bite to eat, get to bed and sleep for a week. And here she was, acting the gamall like the rest of them.

Trying to keep his voice in check he snapped, 'Out o' my way, woman!' and stalked in, but if he did Máire was gone equally quickly by the back door. He was left to stare at her as she hared madly towards a neighbour's house, faster, in fact, than he had ever seen her move before.

He made no attempt to follow, only slumped wearily on to the sofa and began to consider. Something was most terribly wrong here. He could no longer doubt that. But what? He pulled himself to his shaving-mirror. Maybe he had disfigured his face in a way that was frightening them all.

He almost fell out of his standing when he found looking back at him – nothing at all! He was gone ... or at least not there. Or ... or ... This was too unbelievable to even try to put words on. He looked again. Still gone! But where was he? How could a person just disappear?

It never occurred to him that maybe he had never reappeared.

Not daring even to breathe, he raised his right hand to his face, to feel it for himself. And that was when he spotted it, the blue light where his hand ought to be. But there was no trace of any hand. Only the light.

The lamp! That cursed blue lamp! He shook his arm violently to rid himself of the unwelcome thing. But it would not be removed, no matter what frantic contortions he put himself through in the next few minutes, and they were many and frenzied.

His exertions were violently interrupted when the door was burst in by the boots of several neighbours armed with pikes, screwdrivers and shotguns. And there was Máire behind them, urging them on.

''Twas here only a minute ago. A blue light. Moving, it was. It must be Jack's ghost or maybe a worse thing entirely. Maybe an evil spirit.'

Jack dived under the sofa and lay low while they searched. No point in facing people who were in a mood like that, he told himself. Anyway, what Máire had just said was enough to be going on with, whatever she had meant by it.

They proceeded to scour the kitchen and would surely have found him, but just then the priest strode in in his most business-like robes. Someone, in the midst of all the excitement, had thought to summon him. In a matter of minutes he had worked himself into a fine manful chanting of prayers of ... exorcism, no less!

'Is he out o' his mind, too, like all the rest of 'em? Or who does he think I am? The Devil himself?' Jack gurgled, amazed.

The prayers and the intent behind them could not be mistaken, though. And there could be only one response from Jack: clear out for now, while his pursuers were on their knees and temporarily quiet, and come back later when all the fuss had died down.

Unfortunately, he was not fast enough. As he slithered towards the threshold a less-than-devout kneeler spied the stealthy movement of the light.

'Look!' he bellowed, his finger stabbing towards it. 'He's trying to escape on us!'

'Catch him! Stop him!' shrieked the priest, prayers forgotten for the moment as he scrabbled for the holy water.

'Not if my legs can help it,' Jack spat and charged down the pathway, the devout congregation of a moment before now a foaming mob on his tail.

IT WAS THE BEGINNING of a pattern. From that day on he was hunted from post to pillar by this priest and that, all armed with bell, book and holy water, all intent on being the one to rid the land of Ireland of his unwelcome presence.

And gradually, grudgingly, he was forced to accept the terrible truth poking its finger at him from every ditch and crossroad: there was no going back. He had made his choice. Neither Peter nor the Old One wanted him. Of that he could be certain. But neither did Cratloe, Clare, Ireland or anywhere else in the land of the living. He was trapped in a horrible half-existence, neither man nor spirit.

And so he was condemned to a furtive existence in out-of-

the-way places, appearing at dark and ungodly hours, terrifying all who met him in his little blue light.

So he remains to this day, alone, shunned, a wanderer. And
he will be until the walls of the world collapse at last under the
weight of Eternity.

Seán Ó Duinnín and the Devil

FOR AS MANY generations as the average person has fingers and toes the Claddagh of Galway was famous as one of the most tightly-knit communities in all of Ireland. Nearly every family there made its living from the sea, and experts they were at their business, too, the men fishing while the women gutted, salted and boxed the catch. It was a steady, if dangerous, livelihood and many a ruined countryman trudging the streets of Galway when potato-blight had destroyed his crop envied them their snug homes, their full bellies and the healthy appearance of their children.

One of the longest-rooted families in that village was the Ó Duinníns: they boasted that their first ancestor was the man who met Adam and Eve when those unworthies were flung out of the garden. And if men were inclined to smile at this for a slightly exaggerated claim, they did so privately for, as well as being noted fishermen, the Ó Duinníns also had a fearsome reputation with their fists, boots and gutting-knives, especially when the honour of the clan was concerned.

The years of the Boer War were a time of exceptional prosperity, not alone in the Claddagh but also all over Ireland. Prices were as high as demand could raise them, for the troops had to be fed and it was considered by the powers-that-be that salted herring and mackerel were a mighty incentive to the fighting-man to do his duty best for Queen and Empire. The fishermen of Claddagh, naturally enough, had no argument with such wisdom. Galway boomed in those years and men spent freely.

But hungrier days followed the Treaty of Vereeniging and the coming of peace, as is usually the case, and only when the Great War reared its ugly head did the good times come again. Mightier armies than ever before shook the earth now and every man of all those millions had a hungry mouth. For five years there was no end to the toil in Claddagh. Men and women worked all the hours God sent. Or almost all. For no matter what the hurry, one thing they would not do, either for profit, pressure or patriotism, was to fish on a Friday.

'That's the day Our Saviour suffered for us,' the old people said. 'It wasn't worked in our fathers' time, an' it won't be worked in ours either.'

Outsiders shrugged at these quaint notions, those merchants with contracts to fill fretted, and even the local priests were prepared to intervene and negotiate a dispensation. But the ancients of the Claddagh were immovable. There would be no fishing on Fridays however pressing the need. That was that.

In those troubled times Seán Ó Duinnín, the eldest son of the deep-rooted Duinnín family, was approaching manhood, and a fine young lad he was, too, strong, freckled and handsome, with a manner pleasant and most friendly to young and old alike. The apple of his parents' eyes and the pride of the village, he had already long been accompanying his father on fishing trips, so imagine the shock to those people when early one Monday morning – a morning, moreover, when the mackerel were in the bay – he announced that he was sick and tired of the same old dreary round of constant toil in the one place.

'I want to see a bit o' the world,' he said, 'before I'm too old. That isn't much to ask, is it?'

His parents were speechless, so much so that they were unable to object at first. But his friends were more forthcoming: 'Is it so you're out o' your mind?' they asked him urgently. 'If you go out there now, you'll be called up into some army or another. They're still looking for amadáns to die in France for oul' kings an' Kaisers an' fellows like that.'

But there were others, less friendly or concerned, who ascribed baser motives to him: 'Begod, he's comin' out through the top of himself. Gettin' too important entirely for this place, the Duinníns are.'

Begrudgery was alive and well, even in that neighbourly village.

By a mixture of coaxing and well-directed threats Seán's departure was postponed for a year and more, but by the dawn of the new decade even his parents had become reconciled to what they knew could not be changed: he would go, and there was nothing they could do to prevent it. They even attempted to console themselves by considering the threatening aspect of politics at home: 'Muise, God knows, things isn't lookin' too good at the minute. Maybe he'd be better off out of it for a while.' But this was mere neighbour-talk. In their silent hearts they grieved, never more so than when they saw him off for London at the Great Southern station in Eyre Square on a pleasant May morning in 1920, and there were tears as they waved him out of sight. Turning for home, one thing at least was obvious to his brothers and sister: the old man would not survive this blow to his pride, whatever about their mother. Any father who could not keep his eldest son at home, however the rest of the family might fare, was no man in the eyes of the people of Claddagh, much and all as they might sympathise and be understanding in public.

But, for better or worse, the deed was done. He was gone, and life would have to be got through without him.

Days passed into weeks passed into months. There was no word from Seán. Christmas came and went and it was obvious to the other children that the old couple were suffering, though they did their best to be of good cheer for the season that was in it.

The new year began with a sense of resentment, among his brothers at least: why did he not even write? That would have been little enough to ask. But their anger dissipated for want of someone to vent it on, for Seán did not come. Nor during the next year. Nor the next.

Under the circumstances his father did well to last the four years that he did. But even on the day of his burial Seán put in no appearance, to the grief of his mother, who was now convinced that he too must certainly be dead. The rest of the family had their own thoughts but in order to cause the old woman no greater misery they held their opinions close to themselves.

Ten years drifted between themselves and Seán, and if he ever again entered their minds it was only as a brief irritant, for never a word did they hear concerning him, either alive or otherwise.

Yet, he was far from dead. Quite the opposite, in truth. By dint of hard physical work plus his native Galway gobbiness and by getting to know many of his fellow-countrymen in the great city he survived at first, then gradually began to prosper. Yet, despite this slow inching up in the world there was always a lack in his life, something he could feel but not account for. And the coldness and want of nature in the people of London did little to endear the city to him though he lived among them and profited from their needs. Many a night he tossed in his bed, thinking of the place he had left so many years before, wondering 'Why .. ? If only ..? Whether?' Yet the daily grind, the small but relentless necessities of his routine, slowly submerged all thoughts of any homecoming, froze each impulse to go west again and be at peace with himself where he really belonged.

One thing he never forgot, though: his mother's last shred of advice before he left Galway station and his own reply – 'In

God's name, Seán, keep a hold of your ha'penny, an' mind your religion.'

'I will, mother. Don't ever doubt it.' And failed he had not, for when most of his companions stopped attending church on Sunday, preferring to sleep off Saturday night's revels on this their only day of rest, he always took care to fulfil his promise to his mother, even if he went no farther than the church door and could hardly see the priest, let alone hear him.

Drink enough he did during those London years, but never to stupefaction like other lonely Irish bachelors. For one thing, he still preserved that peasant frugality bred of youthful want – he was never one to pamper himself or to expect pampering of others – and also he was stubborn enough to resent parting with his hard-come-by cash to publicans who would scarcely condescend to trade a few civil words with him as they took his money. He began to look on his Irish drinking-acquaintances as somehow simple, to allow themselves to be held in a vice-grip of work for six days and hangover for the seventh, a downward-sloping treadmill that had only one ending for most: a desolate old age kicking autumn leaves in a local park or cemetery, or sitting huddled on a bench thinking wistfully of a home, family and Ireland long vanished. Oisín and Tír na nÓg. The stories of his youth would come back to him as he watched those old men wither uncared-for, all their years of independence gone, the service they had rendered now counting for nothing at all.

And he would most likely have continued to watch them, pitying, condescending, unwittingly on the same road himself, had not an odd circumstance intervened. He was hurrying homeward towards Twisden Road one grey threatening October evening, a parcel of meat for his supper under his oxter, and had barely turned off South Grove and into Swain's Lane when the skies opened and let down a torrent that seemed to blot out the dismal streetscape through which he was passing. He huddled deeper into his coat and looked about for shelter. No sense in going on. There was still the best part of a mile to be walked. He would be saturated by the time he got to the house.

And then he noticed it. Something he had never seen before: one of the black cast-iron gates of Highgate cemetery was open. Many a time, trudging homewards before now, he had wondered why they were invariably chained and pad-locked. Such a useful short-cut the graveyard would make for people like himself, he had often thought, and, why, even the dead might benefit from some little prayer thrown their way by a grateful passer-by. But no! It was the manner of London-ers to value privacy more than charity. Dead or alive, there was little change in them. All such thoughts he pushed aside now, however, for here was the gate, offering entry on this most horrible of days. Seán slipped between the heavy iron uprights and took the path straight ahead, ignoring left and right. It appeared the shortest route to his destination. Head down, he hurried on, expecting to hear at any moment the muted babble of voices in prayer – for surely it was to admit a funeral that the gate had been opened. Then, as he approached a huge beech tree that marked the centre of the cemetery and the meeting-place of the various pathways, a blue and jag-ged flash of lightning stopped him in his tracks. Instinctively he ducked, then looked up, waiting for the thunder which he knew must follow. Instead, a second bolt of lightning flick-ered across the sky, so close that he thought he could hear it crackle. Or was it the cracking of stricken timber? He had no time to distinguish one from the other, for before he could even think of jumping to safety he was engulfed in, falling with, a bedlam of yellow leaves, slashing branches and what seemed like a scattering of all his wits.

For some moments he lay, senses spinning, while the noises continued, then thinned and died away. He looked about him, dazed, then suddenly upward. A huge branch it was that had been torn from its place. 'An' here I am, under it an' nearly dead inside in a graveyard!' Was God having fun at his expense? Hardly the time for questions now. One warning was enough. He raised himself quickly – 'Nothing broken, thank God, but where's my meat?!' – and squeezed through the cage of boughs that imprisoned him. The rain was still falling, heavier now, but he hardly noticed it. Or the fact the he had just escaped death by inches. He wanted his meat. He had paid a solid half-crown for it and God or anyone else had no right to take it from him. He plunged back into the maze of darkening branches, but it was a futile effort, and soon enough he knew it. Almost crying with frustration – and shock, if he had but known it – he scrabbled about on his hopeless task, then, beaten, stumbled back and sat glowering on a low-set headstone that had little besides its shoulders over ground. Unseeing, angry, he looked about him, then allowed his head to flop down helplessly on to his chest. He swayed this way and that for a few moments and then snapped to full consciousness.

It ... could not be! He leaned forward, squinting through the gathering gloom. Hardly a yard from him stood a grimed marble headstone that had once been white, and on it, in letters of unnatural startling black, the words 'Sacred to the memory of Seán Ó Duinnín, who departed this life September 10, 1856'.

The rest of it he left unread. On hands and knees now, he stared, oblivious to all else. How could such a thing be? A name inscribed in Irish in an English – worse, a London – graveyard! He glanced here and there, squinted to examine this and that stone. Solid English names, every one. Hebson,

Firbank, Capstaff, Newcomb, Henderson, Mayne. Not a single other Irish surname in sight. Just the one and only Seán Ó Duinnín. Something urgent, a little voice growing suddenly louder in his mind, told him to go. Now. Before worse happened. But he could not. Not with his own name staring at him from that sad, once-white stone.

He was jolted back to reality by the deep thud of heavy metal on metal. The gate closing! He would be locked in with his buried self.

'No!' he shouted, stumbling forward, 'Don't leave me here. I'm not dead at all.'

It was a shaken enough verger who stared at him from the street-side of the gate, and his suspicions were in no way lessened by Seán's frantic gibberings. Cautiously he undid the chain and made very sure to keep the gate between himself and this creature from the gloom. Seán dashed past him without even a word of thanks and never paused until he was safe in his lodgings, shivering and panting on the bed.

By the following day, Saturday, he had recovered some of his nerve and already curiosity was beginning to replace fear. He would have to go back, he knew, like it or not, and find out whether his eyes had really been victims of the gloom and rain. Cautiously enough he approached, but in the bustle of Saturday shoppers there was nothing even remotely frightening about the graveyard. It was just one more mouldering oasis of quietness amid the frenzy of city life. And the gate was solidly locked. He walked by the railings to the nearest church, his attention always wandering to the huge beech, to the gravestones round about.

The church door was open, but he did not enter. For he had noted with horror the nameboard outside. 'St Athelstan's Church of England,' it proclaimed. Head sideways, he looked again and read it slowly. He could not at once take the notion in: an Ó Duinnín in a Protestant graveyard? Like turnip-pie and cream, the two things made no kind of sense together. He re-read it, but the letters were unyielding, let him believe or believe it not. But there was nothing to be done. He could not enter a Protestant church, even to enquire about such an important matter as this. That was a reserved sin. And so he turned away, back to his room, with much to think about.

Before the weekend was over he had made the decision that had been eluding him for ten years: he would go back. He belonged in the Claddagh, not here in this godforsaken cold land where he would always be alone, no matter what crowds of people surrounded him. And if one Ó Duinnín could end his life so unnaturally why not Seán himself also? It was a warning, clearly, and not to be ignored. He collected together the money he had saved, sold what he could not carry, and within eight days was back in Galway, to the astonishment of all those who had not laid eyes on him for so long.

But there was no amazement on Seán. It was as if he had never gone away, so quickly did he fall back into the rhythm and routines of his former home-place. All except for one thing: he did not go back to the sea. Yet, every day, at the crack of dawn and again at dusk, he was at the quayside to watch the fishermen come and go, and at other times too, always walking, walking, always silent and alone, as if pondering something deep. He was invited to step aboard the boats of course, and lend a hand if he would, even come and see the places where he and his father had once fished. But always he declined with a little smile or an impatient wave of the hand. Unknown to them all, he had plans of his own, plans which would change each and every one of their lives.

One Friday evening, after he had been a month at home, he announced to his mother that he was going on a journey and that he would be away for a few days. She was aghast.

'Airiú, is it so you're off again, an' you only just home? Where are you going, at all?'

'Only a small bit o' business I have to do, mother. That's all. I'll be back in a week, an' then you'll see something that'll open the eyes o' the crowd around here.' And he smiled mysteriously at his two brothers, who stood by, listening.

He said no more, only took the first train next morning, but to where, no one knew. And true to his word, he strode into the kitchen a week later, a smile on his face almost as wide as the doorway. He sat himself down, beaming, and looked around him, daring them to question him.

'Well? Are you goin' to tell us anything, Seán?' they said at last, impatiently.

'What oul' secret are you makin' of all this, whatever 'tis?'

'Ah,' he sighed happily, 'ye'll see it all before too long. Now, where's the tea?' And he rubbed his hands, full of glee, it seemed, at the prospect of something great about to occur. But a fortnight passed. A month. Nothing happened. Yet Seán seemed to grow more excitable with every passing day, hurrying at daybreak to gaze southward and west along the bay. Neighbours began to look askance at him as though he were unhinged.

'For Ballinasloe he is, the poor lad,' they nodded knowingly. They had seen such things before. 'That'll tell you what England is like. Any Irishman'd be better off starving at home than to go to a cursed place like it.' And it brought a kind of happiness to them, the knowledge that in their own confined world of poverty, their dull resignation, lay some sort of virtue after all.

It came as something of a shock to them, then, to discover that Seán was not so mad as they had supposed. For on January sixth, the feast of the Epiphany, his faith – or oddity – was suddenly vindicated. On that morning his by-now-usual plod along the shore was halted by the sight of a vessel in the bay. But not a local boat. He grinned, and then, as it came closer, leaped for joy. At last! At last! Let them laugh now – if they still had a mind to. He dashed to the quay, a-quiver, as the craft loomed larger and nearer. And when it docked he was waiting, a smile lighting his face.

A tall man leaped ashore and saluted Seán.

'You wouldn't be Seán Ó Duinnín, by any chance?'

'That's myself, indeed. Is this my boat?'

''Tis. An' you're a lucky man. If I had the like of her I wouldn't be long making my fortune.'

Seán grinned. 'I worked many's the sore day for it. In London. I'm waiting for this hour a long time.'

He vaulted aboard, began inspecting the huge trawler from stem to stern and hardly even noticed her crew take their leave. He was disturbed at last from his labour of love only by a growl of voices. On the quay a crowd had begun to gather, curious and admiring. Some fingered her woodwork, estimating her dimensions. Others merely scratched their heads in wonder. Certain it was that no such vessel had ever been seen in Galway before. And here she was now, all Seán's. He smiled to himself, whistled a little tune and went about his business.

Questions there were, of course; hundreds of them. But his answer to all was the same: 'I'm here to make a living. I didn't come back for a holiday. As soon as I can get a crew I'll be out there on the bay an' beyond, an' I won't leave a fish from here to America.'

He laughed, and laughed again, at his own outrageous boast. All the things he had always wished for – that everyone in Claddagh had ever wished for – were about to come to pass.

That same day he announced that he was seeking a crew, and there was no shortage of volunteers, for times were hard and work not easily come by. He picked the best eight of the men who presented themselves, told them to report for service at dawn the following day and went home, content, to his breakfast.

More questions than ever awaited him, for word of his boat had spread. He answered, or half-answered, but his mind was elsewhere – down at the harbour with his beautiful craft. And it was there he spent the rest of the day, making himself familiar with every nook and cranny, checking nets and tackle, all the time watched by a babbling huddle of onlookers. He ignored them all, intent only on preparation for their first day at sea.

Just after dawn next morning they pulled away from the Claddagh, sailed out past Mutton Island to the south, past Black Rock and on south-westward towards Ballyvaughan Bay. Directly north of Black Head they settled themselves at last and cast the nets. And such a day's catch no man there could ever remember having heard about, even from the old people, those who remembered everything.

They returned home early that day, proud and delighted, with room on board for not a pollock more, startling those on shore, who expected them back at the usual time, dusk.

There was wonderment and much gossip when the catch was brought ashore, questions and amazed laughter.

'Lord God, but isn't he the likely man? 'Tis a true saying, "briseann an dúchas tré shúilibh a' chait". You can't beat breeding.'

'Yerra, that's all fine, but, sure, his father did nothing great, what!?' grumbled a begrudger.

'Didn't he let Seán go to England, hah? An' wasn't that what made a man o' him?' replied another.

During that day and the weeks that followed, they discussed his pedigree thoroughly and tried to account for this

'The hoor is enchanted, surely,' said one.

'Not at all,' chimed in another. 'Isn't is a great thing to see a man going up in the world through a bit o' hard work?'

'Yerra, hard work it is, airiú! Sure, wasn't the Duinníns only a crowd o' wasters ever?' growled an old-timer, in the traditional manner of neighbourly dispraise.

Whatever disparaging old chat they might console themselves with, there were few among the young men of Claddagh to listen. They were, one and all, his own brother Cóilín included, queuing for the eight jobs he had promised to whoever pleased him most – for already three of the original recruits had been dismissed – 'Too lazy' – and five extra men were needed to tend the nets alone, so heavy was each day's catch. It was heavy enough, almost, to hide the misgivings that each man felt when Seán told them on that first Thursday evening to be there on the morrow as usual.

'Tomorrow, Seán?' inquired his brother. 'But tomorrow is a Friday. We can't go out on the water on Friday.' The other men nodded. Seán looked them over, then fixed each in turn with a gimlet eye.

'Can't we, now? Well, lads, I have news for ye. This boat is sailing out o' here first thing in the morning. D'ye understand me clear? All I'm saying to ye is be here.' He made no threat, hardly even raised his voice, but all of them knew exactly what he meant.

They scattered then, each man to wrestle with his own fears and conscience. Yet, they were all at the harbour at dawn, though more subdued than usual. Jumpy and irritable, they readied the vessel and soon pulled away from the quay-wall. They did not go unnoticed. A straggle of people was collecting to watch this act of impudent impiety, but far from being upset or intimidated by their presence Seán seemed positively pleased at the attention. He waved pleasantly, then blew them a kiss. But no sign of amusement or recognition came back to him. He shrugged: 'If that's the way of it, boys, ye can stay there an' may the báirneachs an' seaweed do ye a power o' good.' He knew well that the nearest they would venture to the sea that day was to pick those delicacies along the foreshore.

Such details were quickly forgotten about in the business at hand, and that Friday passed off like any other day. If anything, the catch was greater than usual.

'A sure sign that the Man Above – praise an' honour to Him – has nothing against a person making an honest shilling,' was Seán's comment as they sailed home in the gathering gloom.

The prophets of destruction had been busy all that day during their absence: 'That's the last we'll see of any o' that crowd.'

'An' no harm, either. Sure, they mustn't have an ounce o' religion between 'em.'

'True. True! They'll be drownded – if there's any justice at all in this misfortunate world of ours.'

It was with a sense of hurt and disappointment, therefore, that they greeted the laden-down trawler when it docked at ten o' clock that night.

'How could God let it happen?' they snarled. 'Isn't it a pure mockery o' religion? Or is there any Heaven or Hell in it, at all? God forgive us for saying it,' – casting furtive glances towards Claddagh chapel as they voiced these heretic words.

Their theological musings were interrupted by Seán's cheery voice: 'Well, boys, how'd ye like a pollock or two? Or a conger eel?' There were no takers. They turned away, enraged that Seán had called someone's bluff – theirs, maybe – and seemed to win.

'But there'll be another time,' they opined. 'If he thinks he's goin' to make his fortune out o' fishing on Friday he's not a right man, an' that's sure. He'll regret this day's work yet.'

If he did, he never seemed to show it, and none of his crew-men could be brought to criticise his actions, either, for unknown to any but themselves they were each a golden sovereign richer at the end of that day's work and the work of every Friday thereafter, a bonus not to be looked askance at in times so hard.

Weeks, months, passed; Lent came round, and there was more demand than ever before for the huge catches of fish that they landed each day. The matter of Friday fishing as a topic of conversation, even of casual reference, was by now long a thing of the past: people no more even questioned why they had ever held such a foolish, nonsensical belief. Everyone who had a boat had scrambled to be in the action as well as Seán, though few did as well as he.

And yet, all the old fears and superstitions came surging back when, on Holy Thursday evening, Seán announced that it would be business as usual in the morning, Good Friday or no Good Friday. Even Cóilín was shaken. He faced his brother, a look of fear in his eyes. It took him a few moments to put words on his thoughts, but when he did he spoke for the whole crew.

'Look Seán, you're my own brother, an' I'd follow you anywhere, anytime – I'd go to New Zealand with you in a currach. But don't ask me to do this. 'Tisn't right or natural' – he emphasised the words – 'an' I don't want to have to refuse you, so don't ask it o' me.'

The others nodded in silent agreement. Sean sighed, but said nothing.

'We're all thankful to you,' Cóilín continued. 'Every one of us. But there's no sense in trying to put our arm around the whole world. Haven't we enough? Look, the nets could do with a proper going-over, an' there's a plank or two below that a rub o' tar wouldn't go astray on. Wouldn't we be better employed at that tomorrow, Good Friday, than out there?' and his pleading eyes flicked towards the darkening bay.

Without raising any argument, seeming almost to lose interest in the whole conversation, in fact, Seán merely pointed down at where his boots were planted and spoke flatly: 'Lads, be here – here! – tomorrow morning. If ye're not ... ye'll be lookin' for jobs.' There was neither triumph nor regret in his voice, just a quietness that explained full well to them that he meant exactly what he said. He turned away, walked to the boat and saw them no more that night. There was too much to be done in preparation for the morning, and he was the man to do it. Let others talk; his wish, and his only wish, was to do. That was what he was good at, and he knew it.

When he returned home for his supper later his mother was at the door, and straight away Seán knew that Cóilín had told her everything. She scurried towards him, hands held pleading.

'What's this they're telling me about you, Seán, a chroí? Surely be to God you're not going fishing on Good Friday.'

He pushed in past her without answering, sick and tired of this constant questioning. 'Mother, will you gimme my supper, an' stop talking!'

She planted herself in front of him and seemed to spit fire.

'You'll get no supper, or anything else in this house until you answer my question for me. Are you going out tomorrow or not?'

Her voice was ratty.

He paused an instant, then smiled.

'Mother, would I do something like that to you? You know me better than that, surely.'

It was an approach that had worked well for him many

times before, this fond son routine. And now it seemed to do its work again. She faltered.

''Tis hard to know anyone in the times that's in it,' she sighed. 'Sure, the whole world is gone mad.'

But, then she rounded on him and asked him squarely, 'But, tell me, are you going or not?'

'Yerra, what? 'Tis fairy-stories you're listening to, mother. Look' – and he clapped his paws on her shoulders, smiled his first-communion smile – 'times is tough an' many a young lad is going to England. Mother, sure you wouldn't want to see me going to that cursed place again.'

Her whole aggressive manner changed, collapsed.

'Oh, Seán, don't be talking! Stay away from it, will you? Cóilín, talk to him, talk to him! Don't let him go away again.'

'Will you shut up!' snarled Cóilín, but he knew that the damage had been done. There would be no help from that quarter now. Seán had made his point.

Supper was eaten in an uneasy silence, and afterwards Seán smoked no more than half his usual pipe of tobacco before rising, bidding them a good night. At the loft door he turned. 'Five o'clock, mother. No later. Call me.'

The old woman was up at the crack of dawn. She had had a hard night of it, worry and prayer shaking her by turns, trying to think of a way to keep him from the sea on this one day. But all in vain. Here arrived was the fatal morning and she was as far away as ever from any plan.

Absently she prepared a meal of sorts and Seán wolfed it back, hardly even noticing what was in front of him. All his attention was on his day's work, not on minor details like food. He rose almost as soon as he had begun, and brushing crumbs from himself, bustled out. He was back again instantly.

'Where's that bastún, Cóilín?' he snapped. 'Is he up yet?'

No answer.

'Well, by the Lord, I'm not waiting for him. Tell him that if he isn't below at the pier in ten minutes we'll go without him, an' he can stay in the leaba until his toenails grow up his ...' His voice faded. He was gone. Only then did Cóilín appear.

'By God, mother, if he thinks I'm going with him out there today he's gone stiff in the mind.'

The poor woman only shook her head. Such division among her sons she had never expected or wished to see.

Seán stamped to the harbour, muttering to himself.

'Irish people! Could you beat 'em? Complaining when there's no work, an' still they won't take it when 'tis there for 'em. Agh!' – and he spat contemptuously.

But if Cóilín had been a problem, there was worse to greet him when he got to the boat. The crew was not there. Yet the significance of it did not dawn on him immediately. He looked around, here, there. No one.

Realisation came to him quickly enough then. They were skulking. He knew it. Refusing to come out because of the day that was in it. But, by God, he wasn't going to take this kind of oul' nonsense from 'em. To hell with this cursed superstition. A hard lesson was what they needed, and he was the man to provide it.

He scrabbled for his fob-pocket and dragged out his watch, that fine, solid turnip of a timepiece that had accompanied him through thick and thicker in London all those years in exile. The very feel of it steadied him. He clasped its bulk between strong fingers, raised up his face, and in a cold colourless voice rasped to the faceless houses, 'Where are ye, ye useless liúdramáns? If ye're in it answer me now or ye'll regret it!'

No answer.

'All right.' He gritted his teeth. 'If that's the way 'tis with ye, we'll see who's the man around here.'

Only echoes answered him, mocking echoes of his own words.

'I'm telling ye now' – and he snapped open the watch – 'if ye're not out here in front o' me in two minutes, ye're fired, ye bastúns.'

Still the windows gaped blankly back at him. But nothing stirred, though from the corner of each and every one his smallest movements were being closely observed.

The seconds ticked relentlessly by. Seán looked around him one last time.

Nothing.

He snapped the watch shut.

'That's my last word to ye, boys,' he snarled. 'Stay there, then, an' be damned to ye for a flock o' cowardly oul' women.'

'Oho, you pagan, you, an' maybe 'tis yourself that'll be damned,' they muttered.

Seán whipped around savagely, strode to the boat and clattered aboard. But he was no more than there when he began to calm down and assess his position. Without a crew he was in trouble. He could not sail her alone, yet if he remained in harbour now, after the commotion of the last few minutes, all his authority would be gone. Those cowardly fools would know that he was in their power whenever they chose to put a squeeze on him.

But where was he going to get five or six men at such short notice, capable men, too?

He was still standing, hands in his pockets, trying to think, when a deep rumble of a voice at his elbow made him jump almost out of his boots: 'What's keeping a fine boat the like o' this idle here, Seán, a bhuachaill, an' the pollock – rakes of 'em – out there waiting to be caught?'

'Wh – who in the name o' Heaven are you, an' where'd you come from?' spluttered Seán, rattled. 'An' how d'you know my name? I never in my life laid eyes on you before.'

The man he was looking at was relaxed, smiling and big. Very big. So big, in fact, that he towered head and shoulders above him, and Seán was no dwarf!

'How d'you know my name, I'm asking you?' repeated Seán, a little less jumpy now, though no less amazed.

'Yhera, Seán, doesn't everyone know you, the man that fishes the seven days o' the week, even a day like this?' and his eyes glittered above his huge toothy smile.

Seán was not smiling.

'Well, I won't be fishing this Friday, an' that's for sure.'

'Why so, my poor man?'

Seán was too taken up with his own problem to notice the tone of that voice.

'Them cowardly bastúns I have for a crew, they won't stir outside their doors, bad cess to 'em.'

The big man smiled more broadly than before and scratched a large brown paw up and down his cheek.

'Well, well! Isn't that the pity o' the world, now? But, look, I wouldn't worry too much about 'em if I was you.'

'That's very easy said when you're not me, but you don't know the trouble that this day's work is going to make for me ...'

'Heh! Heh!' The big man laughed, and it was more than just a laugh. It held promise of something ... something untoward, even unwanted. 'Look, Seán, my boy, I wouldn't let that come between myself an' whatever it was I had to do. Everything can be got around, if the price is right.'

His tone was genial, helpful, in the manner of a cattle-jobber, but Seán had ears only for the hint it offered of a solution to his dilemma.

'How d'you mean? Amn't I telling you that they won't stir?'

'Don't mind that crowd.' The big man's hand swept a contemptuous arc downward and away behind him. 'They don't matter any more. What would you want with 'em when you have a new crew all ready to go?'

Seán paused. New crew? He looked about him but could see no one. No one except the big man. And he was smiling now more broadly than ever, his hands on his hips, waiting.

'I don't ...'

'Look, Seán,' continued the stranger, 'I have a question for you. An' 'tis this. What'll you give me if I do the work of your seven men? Will you pay me seven men's wages?'

Seán looked at him suspiciously. Was the fellow mad? He certainly seemed sane enough. And strong enough. But the work of seven men? Was there a man alive in Galway – or in Ireland – who could do it?

He glanced at the boat, still idle and swaying gently at its moorings, then at the houses. Still no sign of life. He shrugged. Better to humour him. Sure, there was nothing to be lost since the day was lost anyway. And he had always liked a challenge.

'All right. Let you prove to me that you can do it an' I'll pay you what you're worth.'

'Oh, don't have no fears about me. What I say I'll do. Get your stuff an' we'll go, so. Now!' And he rubbed his hands together gleefully. It sounded too like an order for Seán to be wholly comfortable, but it was too good an offer to refuse, a chance to teach his idiot crew a lesson.

'You're hired,' he smiled. 'Go on aboard an' make ready. I have to go back to the house an' tell herself I'm going out. I won't be long.'

'Don't!' and he turned smartly and tramped off towards the quayside.

Seán hurried home, a new spring in every step. The old woman met him at the door. He clapped his hands on her shoulders, then broke the good news.

'You'd never believe what happened me below there, a mháthair!'

She did not reply. Obviously she was not at all curious to hear his story, whatever it might be. He crushed in past her, still smiling, and went about collecting together his various bits and pieces. In a little heap at the door he piled them, then straightened up ... and only then noticed her standing stock-still where he had left her.

'Look, mother,' he said breezily, 'while you're standing there doin' nothing else wouldn't it be the one thing for you to make a drop o' tea for me before I go?'

The words seemed to have a magical effect on her, for she came to life of a start.

'Go? You'll go no place today,' she screeched. 'Not a step more from this house will you take. On Good Friday? Are you out o' your mind, or what?'

'Look, mother,' he replied wearily, 'I heard all this before. I'm going out fishing, an' that's that. Will you make the tea, for God's sake, or will I have to do it myself?'

'I'll make no tea for a pagan. If you want a drink, go down an' throw yourself into the harbour. That'll bring you to your senses.'

He sighed, eyes to heaven. Mothers! Was this the only reason they were put in the world, to stand in the way of their sons? Yet, he could not let her words go without reply.

'I won't say no more to you now, woman. But I never broke my word yet. Once I have a bargain made I'll keep it, whatever else, so stand out o' the way if you're going to be no help to me.'

'What bargain, you amadán? What're you after doing? Tell me!'

She was becoming more agitated by the moment, spurred on, perhaps, by the sound of her own voice rising. But he was no longer listening. Instead he grabbed her.

'Come here!' he snapped, dragging her roughly to the door.

'D'you see that man below, sittin' on the boat?'

She tried to focus, but for all her squinting she could not make him out, and well Seán knew it.

'What about him? Who is he?'

'I don't know his name, an' I don't care. But he's the one I made my bargain with an' we'll be sailing once I have the tea drank an' that stuff there at the door loaded.'

At that moment Cóilín's head appeared around the jamb of the room door, but before he could say a word Seán got in a quick gibe: 'Oh? An' you're up, are you? Well, Cóilín, boy, you can go back to sleep now. I have someone got that'll do what you wouldn't. An' you can tell the same thing to the rest of 'em when you meet 'em.'

His voice was anything but brotherly and the fact was not lost on Cóilín, for he merely scowled, disappeared for a few moments, then emerged, pulling on his trousers as he came.

'I don't know where you think you're goin', boy, but 'tisn't with me you're travelling, anyway,' said Seán harshly.

Cóilín did not reply, only struggled to the door and peered long and intently towards the harbour. When he turned again to Seán there was an odd look on his face, as if he had seen some wonder. He shook his head; then, hand to his forehead, he looked out again.

Seán watched him and smiled, a grim smile. 'Faith, Cóil, if you think you're goin' to work any of your oul' tricks on me with the way you're actin' ...'

'Come here, quick', whispered Cóilín, 'an' tell me am I seein' things. What in the name o' Heaven's door is that thing below?'

The old woman was first to his side, Seán sidling over more slowly. He still suspected Cóilín of some kind of trickery, but the look on his mother's face now told him that something was not as it should be.

His boat! His precious boat! Was ..? The thought cata-pulted him to where they stood gaping, his mother clutching tightly at Cóilín's arm.

But ... there was nothing! All was as he had left it: harbour, boat, and the new man smoking peacefully by the rail.

He wheeled on them.

'What oul' codology are ye going on with this time?' he snarled. 'Is it tryin' to put the heart crossways in me ye are?'

His mother turned. In her eyes was fear, and a cold grey look on her face. Cóilín, likewise, was ashen. A bony old hand scrabbled for Seán and in a cracked voice she stammered out: 'God in Heaven preserve us, but don't tell me you sold your-self to that fellow, to the Dark Lad himself!' Her fingers were trembling.

As if he were dealing with some type of simpleton, Seán gaped, then snatched his hand away.

'Enough o' this ráiméis. I'm off, fishin'. This cursed place is gone stone mad.'

'Can't you open your eyes an' see what's there below waitin' for you? Look at the cloud o' black smoke around him, an' the big hairy tail he has, an' the horns!'

There was pity in Seán's voice as he answered her.

'Mother, 'tis time you got glasses. I'll take you to the doctor above on Taylor's Hill when I come back from this trip. An' maybe I'll get a pair for you, too, Cóil,' he sniggered, and was gone, snatching up his belongings as he went.

'Wait, Seán! Wait,' she screamed, dashing after him. 'Don't go. I never asked you to do much for me before now, but if you'll only stop in today, an' keep away from the water, I'll never again put a word in your way.'

'I have talking enough done for one day, mother. My man

below won't wait forever, so stand back now an' don't be both-
erin' me.'

Like a faithful old dog unwilling to be ordered back home,
she followed him, begging, pleading, praying, always glancing
furtively and in growing panic towards the quay.

When she saw at last that his ears were closed to all her
pleas she clasped his arm and attempted to drag him around
to face her.

'Seán! Seán! Listen to me. Only one word ...'

He shrugged her off, never slackening his stride.

'Seán, d'you remember that day at the station when you
were goin' to England?'

He paused, then glanced down at her.

'What about it?'

'D'you remember the advice I gave you that day?'

He still walked on, but this time he made no reply.

'Seán, I wouldn't put the bad word on you. All I want is
for you to come back safe, an' if you go out today you won't do
that. The lad below, he'll be the finish o' you. Of that I'm sure
an' certain.'

Maybe the memory of that distant day's parting, or a stab
of guilt at never seeing his father alive again, struck him now.
Whatever it was, he saw before him a frail old woman, bent
and wrinkled, he knew, at least partly by his negligence. He
owed her much. That was obvious. But what could he do
about it now? Yet his pace slowed. And she was still speaking,
begging.

'... an' if you'd only take this with you, at least, maybe we
might see you again on dry land.'

He stopped. Her left hand was raised almost to his face, and
clasped between the cracked and pitted nails was her crucifix,
the rest of the rosary-beads out of sight, hidden in her fist.

'Will you take this with you, at least? Your father – God

149

rest his soul – he gave it to me the day we were married, an' it won't bring you any bad luck.'

'All right, mother,' he sighed. 'If it'll keep you happy,' then silently, 'an' let me get on with my business.'

With a smiling face but yet with shaking hands she draped the beads over his head and round his neck, then tucked the crucifix down inside his shirt.

'Keep a tight hold o' that when trouble comes, a chroí, an' you won't go far astray.'

'I will, I will, o' course, mother,' he soothed, anxious to be off. 'But I must go on, now. Keep the dinner hot for me, will you? I won't be too late.'

And he planted a little kiss on her forehead, disentangled himself deftly from her grasp and skipped off towards the boat, blowing more kisses behind him as he went, the very picture of a happy man.

He dashed aboard and flung a curt order to the 'crew': 'Cast off as fast as you can, an' take your stations!'

The words were out before he saw the ridiculousness of them. But he was used to ordering several men; the habit was an old one. Yet, as never before, his order was obeyed now, for the big man had not to be commanded twice. With one furious wrench on the hawser he dragged with him not only the iron mooring-ring but also the huge limestone block to which it was attached. He grinned as it plunged into the water, but Seán was not so amused.

'Blast it,' he growled, 'is it so you want us to try sailin' with that thing tied to us, hah?'

The big man cocked his head, looked sideways at Seán, then in two swift steps was at the bow, had grasped the rope and ... bit it in two! He allowed the weighted end to coil over the side, held up the frayed remainder and leered.

'Well, cap'n, are you satisfied now?'

He went about his duties then, leaving Seán to stare after him open-mouthed and wondering. His mother's words whispered in his mind and his fingers wandered uneasily to her beads. But the big man's work thereafter dulled his unease somewhat for he went about his tasks with an enthusiasm that was frightening in its efficiency but at the same time positively fascinating to Seán. In a flurry of hauling, heaving and grunting, he did all that the eight previous crewmen had done, and did it more tastefully, far more thoroughly.

'Holy God,' thought Seán, 'who'd be without a man like that? Isn't he a wonder entirely?'

The long and short of the story was that for the first time in his fishing career Seán did not lift a finger on the voyage out of Claddagh. For once he could stand and observe all the landmarks of the bay on this most delightful of mornings – Tawin Island and Kilcolgan Point, Finavarra and Aughinish further south, and away in the distance Black Head.

He felt faintly guilty, felt almost like one of those odd useless fellows who had been seen of late in Galway on their way to the west, to learn Irish, talk about times gone by to toothless old relics, or something equally senseless. But there was nothing for him to do. The big man was in complete control, moving here and there with an ease that was all-too-obviously practised.

'Who'd he work for before this? If he's so good, why isn't he his own boss? Begod, maybe the poor man has a drink problem, or trouble with the wife – if he has one. Or he could be ...'

A hundred such notions passing through his mind kept Seán occupied until at last the man stepped up, tapped him on the shoulder and offered: 'We're here, cap'n. The best fishing-ground in all Galway Bay, you'll find – I think.'

Seán blinked, glanced around. 'Hah? Oh, yes, yes! Well ... we better let down the nets, so. Wouldn't it be as well?'

'Oh, whatever you say, cap'n, a chroí,' and as he spoke he

was already bundling them over the side at a speed which left Seán breathless. Not a word passed his lips while the work was a-doing, and even less was he inclined to talk as they waited for the fatal meshes to do their silent work.

But their wait was an incredibly short one, for in the space of a few minutes there was a trembling of all the plank-work, as if some great hand had them in its grasp, then a sharp yaw to starboard. Seán came alive of a flash.

'God almighty, it must be a whale that has us. Cut the nets, there, quick' – and he tossed his long-bladed knife to the big man, who caught it, looked at it an instant and then let it clatter to the deck.

'I'm surprised at that kind o' talk from a man o' the Duinníns. Cut the nets! There's a change in the world, surely, since I was here last,' and without more explanation he began to haul the nets aboard, mesh over mesh. And hardly a single one of all that multitude of cords came up without a fish. Seán watched, transfixed as the greatest catch he had ever seen unfolded itself before him, dragged aboard by those muscular arms. Hundreds there must be, thousands even. His eyes danced and in his mind clinked the money he would earn from this mighty day's work.

Soon the deck was awash with a glittering mass of flapping fins and tails. Seán waded through them to the tiller, chuckling, his mind completely immersed now. Mechanically he went through the routines of swinging the boat around to prepare for the trip back, hardly noticing that the big man was no longer here, there and everywhere. The sluggishness of the weighted-down craft was what alerted him to some subtle change. He looked about, and there, sitting at the point of the stern, was his friend, hands spread out along the rail at either side of him and a cigarette, no less, dangling from the corner of his mouth. But it was his attitude of defiant insolence that sobered Seán.

'Hi! What the hell d'you mean, thrown down there slinge-ing an' plenty work to be done? What d'you think I'm paying you for?'

The big man slowly removed the cigarette and glared at him.

'That's the bother, cap'n. You're not payin' me. In fact, the more I think of it, maybe you should gimme my wages now.'

His eyes never left Seán's face all the while he was speak-ing.

'But how in the name o' God can I pay you now – unless you want to start eating raw fish? Have a small splink o' sense, man. Wouldn't it be a lot more in your line to get off o' your backside an' rise up the sails – or better again, start rowing, if you think you're as good as the eight men that were here before you.'

Seán's courage was returning as his annoyance grew.

'C'mon, shift yourself. We're hardly moving, an' it'll be all hours o' the night before we're home at this rate o' going.'

The big man studied him, blew out a cloud of smoke and then flicked the cigarette over the side, half-unsmoked. He levered himself up, ran his fingers through his hair and with a cold little smile – or a grin? – turned from Seán and started to hoist the sails. Seán took the helm, quietly confident now that there would be no further delay and that he would dock in time to let Cóilín and the others savour their foolishness in not sailing today. He could picture them, their efforts to hide their disgust and disappointment at his great day's work.

The big man had begun to see the light, too, it seemed, for as soon as all was in proper trim he returned, saluted and smiled.

'Not much of a breeze, cap'n, but I won't be long fixing that.'

Before Seán could even gather his thoughts to wonder what this might mean he had turned, faced the mast and begun to inhale. To Seán's utter amazement he did not stop as a normal man would when his lungs were full, but kept gobbling in draught after draught of air, swelling up all the while like some grotesque rubber figure. He bulged across the width of the deck and, when it seemed he must surely burst, he turned a hideous and horribly misshapen face towards Seán and croaked evilly: 'Now cap'n, I'll have my wages, whether you like it or not.'

He began to blow then, gust on mighty gust of foul breath, up from the depths of himself, filling the sails and spreading such a stench that Seán felt his guts churning. Nothing he had ever experienced before – dead animals, stinking fish, cesspits – could equal this for vileness. Even the fish still quivering in the nets caught it, and died at once.

Seán could only clasp his nose, try to prevent himself from vomiting, and watch, terror-stricken. In the space of seconds a blackness fell on the boat and the wind rose into a gale, then a very hurricane. Mast and spars cracked, were bent almost to breaking-point and Seán was on the point of screaming, 'Stop!' when he was flung over, then back across the deck, slithering, tripping, his hands grabbing for support.

A final mighty blast of air and the boat could take no more. It keeled to port, and Seán found himself sliding, falling, together with his precious catch, towards the water.

'No!' he bawled, desperate but by now helpless. 'You can't do this! These are my fish, every one of 'em,' and he threw his arms out to stop the slide to destruction. But it was a hopeless gesture. He might as well have been trying to hold back an avalanche. The slimy mass engulfed him, swept him screaming over the side and head-first into the icy water of the bay. The last fleeting images he took with him as he went under were a bellow of evil laughter from the stern and a glimpse of a wide mouth in a wider face and two rows of yellow teeth grinding.

He struggled desperately to free himself from the debris that bore down on him, and when at last he spluttered to the surface a scene of desolation greeted him. The boat was gone. Only dead fish, a few bobbing boxes and lengths of rope remained to tell of the dream that had been Seán Ó Duinnín's.

But first things first. Regrets later. He kicked off his heavy boots and began to swim, beating his way towards a cluster of small rocks that pushed their seaweedy heads out of the water fifty yards away. He pulled himself onto one, shivering, teeth chattering between curses and moans. But he had hardly seated himself on that comfortless perch when a loud splash somewhere behind him made him turn. There, to his horror, he saw the big man rising in a foam of spray from the depths, shoulders ... chest ... waist ... knees ... feet, until he was standing squarely on the water as though it were solid under him.

Seán gaped stupidly at where his own legs hung submerged to the knees, then back to the horrible figure looming, hands folded, smiling.

Then it spoke, and to Seán the words spelled doom.

'My payment, Ó Duinnín! I want my payment now.'

'God wither you,' stammered Seán, 'you took my boat, didn't you. An' my grand catch. What more d'you want?'

'Is that what you call payment, a few oul' broken boards an' dead fish? Is it trying to make little o' me you are?'

'Well known you hadn't to slave hard in London for the same broken boards, as you call 'em, you bad-minded bod-ach.'

The big man's face clouded darkly; his grin changed to a snarl.

'I have talking enough done to you, my boyo. But now your bill is due, an' I'm taking what's owed to me – yourself!'

His huge paws arched out towards Seán, fingers like talons, and he began to stride across the water. Seán saw his end staring him most surely in the face unless some miracle

... and then he remembered it! The rosary-beads his mother had draped around his neck. It was his only chance now. Chilled fingers scrabbled to open his top button, failed, then ripped it off entirely. The rosary, praised be God, was still there, cold but comforting, though the sharp edge of a small doubt pricked itself in at that moment: how had he ignored it before now? But he dismissed the thought. It mattered not at all how. It was there, and it was his one possibility of escape ... he hoped! Rising shakily, he snatched the crucifix, jerked it up and out, breaking the chain in the process. The ogre was no more than two steps from him now, hands clutching. The crucifix, held so tightly between Seán's frozen fingers, five beads hanging trembling to it, looked tiny and helpless as he measured the giant against its cross-beam. Arm held out rigid, he turned his head away, closed his eyes and tensed, expecting the worst.

There was a splash, a muffled gurgle, then an animal snarl of anger, rising to pain. He peeped. To his astonishment the big man was cringeing, beginning to turn away, his palms held to his face as if for protection. His great feet began to churn the water as he tried to reverse, to escape, it seemed.

'Stop! Keep that cursed thing out from me. Keep it back!'

His voice rose higher with every word. Seán needed no more information. His mother. God bless her. She had been right.

'You can take your pay now,' he cried, almost boldly. 'Here!' – stabbing the cross forward – 'There's nothing like something holy for the likes o' you.'

Inches from the terrifying little object the Devil – for who else was it but he? – managed to stop, but only for an instant. As if burned, he twisted himself around and made off in a series of leaps, his yells echoing across the bay, drawing thunder from the very clouds.

Seán gasped and stared motionless as the huge fellow beat a path westward, yelping, sending spray and foam in showers onto the Clare and Connemara coasts. The last he saw of him was when he jumped out across the Aran Islands, on his way, obviously, towards the broad Atlantic and America.

It was a few moments before quiet rolled again over the waves. When it did it found Seán shivering on his perch, still pointing like a signpost, and colder than he could ever remember. The lapping of the waves against his legs it was that aroused him from his stupor. At once he sat down – straight to his waist in water. The tide! It had turned and was in full flow. Without a second thought he heaved himself forward and swam for land and life, dazed yet conscious that he must, above all else, make it to that green hill of Seaweed Point which he could just make out in the distance. It was the one landmark he recognised at that moment.

Whether he would have reached shore without the help of the two planks that so obligingly floated across his path it is not possible to know. All that concerned his mother, himself and his neighbours was that he did arrive, though more dead than alive. How many hours he lay among the stones and wrack neither he nor the young boys who discovered him knew; his first inkling that he was still among the living came when he found himself being carried on a door by Cóilín and three other of his crew, his mother trotting alongside clutching his hand. And there were faces on all sides. Staring. Silent.

As the door of his own house closed on the gathering crowd, darkness lapped over him once more and he remembered nothing else until he awoke in his comfortable bed, friends by his side and a cup of hot tea in his mother's hand for him.

And when he walked abroad again a week later there were questions – but all of them frozen to the faces of those he met.

No one asked him directly what had happened there beyond in the bay, not to mention the more tempting and delicious notion of 'why?' Yet it was the topic of all conversation, not alone in Claddagh but in the town of Galway, too – after Mass, at the market and in the dark snugs of Cross Street, High Street and Lower Dominic Street, and though there were some who voiced their sympathy that Seán had been brought low – 'God damn it, but wasn't the man tryin' to do something that was never tried before'? – most felt that right had triumphed and that God had shown Himself not only all-powerful but just also. And among these was Seán's own mother. But as Seán well knew (in spite of the matter of the rosary-beads), that was why mothers were put in this world in the first place: to stand in the way of their sons.

Sometimes.

Whatever about that, there was no more Friday fishing in the Claddagh afterwards. The clergy read it most thoroughly from the altar as the Devil's own work. And for once they had the complete support of all the people.

Not surprisingly, even to this very day that custom remains.

Glossary

A bhuachaill:	Boy. Affectionate interjection
A chroí:	My dear. Affectionate interjection
A mháthair:	Mother
Airiú:	Ah! Interjection
Amadán:	A fool
Báirneachs:	Limpets
Bastún:	A person without sense
Bodach:	An ignorant person
Briseann an dúchas tré shúilibh a' chait:	Breeding breaks through the eyes of the cat
Cabaire:	A person too smart for his own good
Céilí:	A social session with music and dancing
Ciaróg:	A black beetle
Cníopaire:	A miserable person
Crúb:	A foot or hand
Currach:	A small boat
Dreamall:	A very small amount of liquid
Dúidín:	A short-stemmed clay pipe
Gamall:	A senseless person
Leaba:	A bed
Liúdramán	A lazy, useless person
Mo léir:	Alas
Muise:	Well, well! Interjection
Óinseach:	A foolish woman
Poitín:	Home-distilled liquor
Ráiméis:	Nonsense
Scairt	Burst
Slán go fóill, a dhuine:	Goodbye for the moment, my friend
Sliotar:	A hurling ball
Yerra:	Interjection expressing indifference, disbelief, etc.